Beula Kettlehole and The Patriarchal Ice

Frontispiece

Lady weeping at the Crossroads
Would you meet your love
In the twilight with his greyhounds
And the hawk on his glove?

W.H. Auden. Collection, 1940

Kettle Hole During the melting stages of the continental glaciers of the Pleistocene Period, large masses of ice were embedded in the stratified drift. The melting of these huge ice blocks resulted in the slumping of the loose material to form well-defined and steep-sided depressions...

from Van Nostrand's Scientific Encyclopedia, 4th Edition, p. 969

Beula Kettlehole and The Patriarchal Ice

Barbara P. Parsons

Writers Club Press
San Jose New York Lincoln Shanghai

Beula Kettlehole and The Patriarchal Ice

Writers Club Press
an imprint of iUniverse.com, Inc.

For information address:
iUniverse.com, Inc.
620 North 48th Street, Suite 201
Lincoln, NE 68504-3467
www.iuniverse.com

ISBN: 0-595-13522-6

Printed in the United States of America

To my husband Jim

PART ONE

1

Broadway, 1973

"Let me take care of this. Will you pass me that telephone? Mmm yello. Yes, is this Emergency? A woman here on Broadway screaming her head off. Listen to this. Got a strong pair of lungs ain't she? No, only one woman. Age? Anyplace between thirty and sixty. Identification? Wait. Pass me that bag under her shoe. I'm looking in the pocket book now. No I don't see no credit cards. Nope. No driver's license. No ID. Ask the woman her name. Hey Mam, what's your name? I can't get through to her. Insurance? Do you see a card? We don't see a card. Social Security card? I'm looking. Make a space here, I can't see what I'm doing." The speaker, Irv Pozzack, passed a hand over his well-combed hair and glared up at onlookers crowding the entrance to his used-furniture store.

"What we got here? Lemme see, there's a makeup sachet, a coin purse with keys and change, a wallet with photographs, a receipt from Red Apple, a paper bag with catfood."

A bystander spoke up, "She's a foreigner. I heard her speak. Australian. That's why she got no credit cards."

Irv continued, "No library card, no letter addressed to her. Nah, I told you, nothin'. Cash? A couple of singles. Checkbook! I'm telling you, *bubkes*."

"She could have a telephone number," said a West Indian woman in a business suit.

"Ask her for a telephone number," another suggested.

"She's sobbing now," the woman said.

Setting the telephone down, Abe Pozzak came out of the store and knelt down beside his brother, "I tell you she's incomunicado," he said, "Here comes the police."

A blue and white police car slid to a stop at the curb. Two officers got out and ambled over—parting the crowd with their presence—to the spot where the woman lay, her head resting on a burgundy seat cushion. Her chignon had got unwound.

"Careful not to step on her hair," said the West Indian woman, carefully smoothing it down and tucking it under her shoulder, wiping the collapsed woman's brow with a witch hazel pad, "There there. There there."

"What's with this woman?" A frowning Officer Kunick addressed Irv Pozzak, "This your store?"

"It's my store. The woman comes by looking for a mirror and starts screaming and carrying on right outside."

"She never came into the store?"

"Like I told you, officer, she stood on the sidewalk and started yelling."

"Aha. And what is this coffee cup doing laying here with the lipstick on it?"

"My wife was here," said Irving, nudging his brother.

"Aha. Aha," Officer Kunick walked up to the oak breakfront and back, "And why is the woman sobbing and moaning? Has she been shot?"

"Shot! Not as far as I know, officer. I didn't see no blood anyplace."

"You gonna have to get her into an ambulance. Here, if the hospital doesn't respond, call this number. We got an urgent call, an old man about to jump off a roof ten blocks north," He extended his walkie-talkie aerial, "OK 746374, we're on our way. We stopped for a vagrant on Broadway and 84th Street."

"I'm worried, Irv," Abe said, "I did not contribute to this."

"Calm down, will you? Thank you, I'll hold. Yeah, yeah, yeah. East side of Broadway. Middle of the block. Yeah. You can't come? What's up, don't you have a vehicle ready? They don't have an ambulance ready."

"Irv, this is an emer-gen-cy."

"They won't come. Why won't you come? Yeah. yeah. yeah. Aha. Yeah. They won't come. And the why is. They don't know how they're gonna get paid."

"How much do they say it's gonna be for Christ sake?"

"They figure with collection and hospitalization it could run to eighteen thousand, not to mention possible surgery."

"When she came into the store she didn't look right but she didn't look sick either."

An older man with a shopping bag said, "So, how come she looks sick now?"

"Wait, she's stopped," the West Indian woman bent down and said softly, "What is your name?"

"It's…it's…"

"Julia is it? Now Julia can you hear me? Is there a telephone number we can call to get help?" She got down in a crouching position and waited. After a bit the woman looked up.

"'Yes,' she says. What's the number? Quick, write it down. It's seven two six, four six three one. Wait, it may be four six three nine. Is it four six three nine?"

Beula whispered in the ear of the woman bending over her, "I came up against something. The mirror. Things weren't good before that. They were—unbearable. Then it all sweeps over me."

"Lie still now. Don't tire yourself out talking."

"If I only felt right, psychically."

"What she say?"

"She wants to feel okay."

A young man with curly hair crouched down as the West Indian woman got up. He took out a rumpled but clean handkerchief and, making a pad with it, began wiping the tears and sweat, working across her eyebrows and down her nose with light swift movements.

"Do you feel more or less okay now?"

"Just now I thought I was close to where okay used to be. But I can't see any signs." She opened her eyes, "Am I still here?"

"You're on the sidewalk. We're waiting for a vehicle to take you to a women's shelter. You just lie still and hang in there now."

I see beggars around, the young man thought. And I've met street people. But they weren't quite like her. Where does somebody like that come from? Now she's moaning. Her hair in disarray, her pallor, her curved eyelids, she looks like at one time she might have been passable-looking, he decided.

2

Bogota, 1971

Ah, that other place, that other avenue. If she could somehow keep it from jumping away, only close her eyes on Broadway and open them to the Carrera, just hold onto the merest sense of it. The Carrera, so like Broadway. So unlike. The Carrera, divided by unfamiliar trees, dwarf hedges, always in leaf. A vista floated up, faded then gradually re-emerged. It must have been one of the days she lunched at La Manuelita, early on in her tour of duty. Waiting to cross on the divider with its privet dwindling to a patch here, a patch there, she'd got used to seeing the gamines at their get-togethers, ducking in and out of traffic, crouched down in a circle, passing a wine bottle.

She'd had no especial fondness for the Carrera, just another dingy, forbidding high-traffic boulevard. Still, it didn't sock it to you. Not a single overflowing garbage basket, not one plastic fork, not a chicken bone, nor even a matchstick between the paving stones. Not that there was any lack of trash but Nolita the maid said it got eaten, fed to pigs, burned, taken back, repaired. Nolita grumbled about shyness with soap and water, partly washed plates, unwashed hands. But to Beula who didn't believe in the force of microbes, it all added to the charm of the place, high up in the eastern cordillera of the Andes, eighty-six hundred feet above sea-level in the rarefied air that played tricks with your short-term memory.

*

The usual film hung on the mountain air that day, a mixture of traffic fumes, soot and grit, suspended in great cells of churning water vapor and puffy banks of cloud, suddenly parting to reveal the sun, first a shiny dinner plate, then with white hot radiance, settling on Beula's blonde head, making it sparkle. She felt in tune with the city that day. Spaces around her had expanded into unending calm that slowed her attention, sliding it into the present. For once she felt neither stuck in the spadework of the morning nor straining ahead to the emptiness of the evening. She was in the here and now, unplagued and airy, so airy that she longed to dance.

Loud cumbia rose up from the little outdoor music stall. Sparkly and flirtatious, she strolled past the three men guarding the stock and, catching the eye of the handsomest, began to move her hips in time to the beat. With a hand against her navel she wiggled to the tune of *Amarillo Color Que Color Color.* Her selected partner sidled over and unsmiling and untouching, glances locked, they wheeled around then made a reverse wheel. A band of men collected on the sidewalk shouting for more but before the end of the number she laughed and shook her head. Supposing the number two had driven by or worse, the boss? "Tengo una sita," she told the men with a wave and a bow so they should have no hard feelings. She knew that being blonde set her apart, in the sense of being beyond reach. Almost. The glances told her they saw a glow wherever she passed.

The city needed a glow for it looked especially brown that midday under the elusive sun, even here at the center where all the wealth was said to be concentrated. Along with the flyblown tobacconist and laid back bar with smoky curtains and uncertain hours, were dingy old showrooms, neither closed, it seemed, nor doing business. Faded advertising cards competing with outdated hi-fi's and 1960's dental equipment.

People in brown or black, not sexy black more like mourning black. Jackets as if folded up in a damp place for months. No miracles were worked with a needle either, judging by tatters worn quite openly. It all added up to local color: Indian women in trilby hats, peddling ponchos in startling reds and greens, strapped to silent black-eyed babies.

Andean paving stones have ways of upending themselves but Beula needed no caution. An open manhole appeared to her at the opposite curb, its cover propped up against a tricycle. She sprang up the steep curb, sashayed round the gaping cavity, meeting the eye of the sewer worker below ground level, flashlight strapped to his head. Giggling, she clip-clopped across the cobbles to the restaurant, wondering about the time. Her platinum wristwatch had drawn quite a few comments, "A bit precious-looking for the office," from her colleague, Elna, known as the Poison Dwarf, she who had gone to school with Winston Churchill's great-niece. It was paradoxical in a country rich in precious stones that one could not wear a single piece of jewelry to lunch, not even a ring. (An acquaintance of the Poison Dwarf's had had a finger chopped off for its emerald.) The story seemed unreliable but Nolita confirmed that only a lunatic like the senora upstairs would wear accessories in the street. Watch, bangles, gold pendant, earrings and purse had to be left in the office locked away.

Jewelry or no, she felt her allure to be intact. Peach patent shoes with flat bows, crisp matching linen frock, three inches above the knee. Once inside La Manuelita's sustaining atmosphere, chink of glasses, faint laughter, she saw the major domo's eyes light up as, taking her elbow, he piloted her to the usual window on the plaza. Sunlight showed again between riding clouds, making little suns on the cocktail trolley. A bus-boy came to fill her water glass and leave a basket of banana bread. The old man couldn't steady his hands and when he poured from the carafe they started to shake in earnest.

The kitchen at La Manuelita never deviated. The *ajiaco* was never too thin, never lumpy. Last week, her waiter, Jorge, had murmured, 'What beautiful hair,' as with a flourish, he slid the bowl of milky soup before her. Sunlight, bathing one side of the plaza, did not light up the eyes of the vendors or of the beggar with the crooked spine. Their faces stayed closed, saying, "I was expecting a dull day. I dressed for it and I don't want my mood changed."

"Would the senorita like coffee now?" Even the mild blend made your arms tingle if you drank more than three a day. Was that due to the *tinto* or the altitude? But she'd have to wait until three thirty when Luisito served tea in the Delegation which, by the time it got to the female staff had been so clobbered with water that, yes, she might indulge in a cappuccino with cinnamon. Sitting over creamy rice with yucca she gazed at the to-ing and fro-ing in the square.

The cathedral struck the half hour. The beggar bent nearly double with a sack of bottles and jars, put down his load and rested on a wall. Suddenly she didn't feel light any more. It was the let-down feeling that follows a meal. What's the point in lingering when there's no one to linger with? She took the *cuenta* from its brass plate and tiptoed out. A merengue filtered down from an amplifier high in the corner. Jorge, the waiter, poised beside the cashier's desk, rolled his eyes at her.

"Not dancing today, senorita?"

She crinkled her eyes and holding a hand out in front, wiggled to the beat. This was his cue to join in, but he looked beyond her to a party of latecomers, lovely, fragile girls of nineteen, smelling of hair salons, dressed in pure silk pant suits, somber blues and golds, highlighting their large eyes and pale skin. Their escorts, young hidalgos in tweed and velvet stood about, flicking cigarette ash on the carpet.

The cashier-owner of the establishment took his time finding change for a young woman who had pushed in front of Beula and was waving a five hundred peso note. He unlocked a steel box riveted to the desk. Not only did he have insufficient change, he had no cash float. She's not pretty, Beula noted, as she watched the girl rooting about in her sacklike bag for a twenty. Her forelip looks taller than her forehead.

Abstracted, she stared ahead through the gloom at an older woman. The face, a little out of shape. Desiccated. Beula sometimes traced with a finger the lines of magazine celebrities to search out qualities like humor, firmness, resignation. A split-second glance at this face told all. Shadows round the eyes told of dread; in the eyes themselves submission, conflict; lines from nose to mouth poised for flight; sensuality as a place to hide.

A coin purse rode up in the swell of objects in the young woman's handbag and in that instant, as Beula took out her wallet, the whole wall became a mirror. The older figure was herself.

*

In a lightning shift of expression the spectacle gave way to the self she knew, eternally twenty-seven, not only abloom but ethereal, from another part of the cosmos. The shock had deadened as it went in, the unwanted image sinking down among sediments of occlusion. In the reassurance that the moment was no revelation, she nodded an adios at the owner. Yet she felt far from all right making her way back to the Delegation offices over the manhole and open drain, navigating by remote control.

As luck would have it, the office elevator was out of order. Gasping, she got to the seventh floor where the hall clock pointed to five minutes past three. To make matters worse, the Senior Trade Delegate, Willis Grapnel, and entourage crowded the entrance, spilling over into the lobby. His principal assistant, Camber Phuff, close behind the chief, stood legs apart, looking at the ground, then the two bodyguards with a canvas bag between them and, in the rear, the chauffeur holding the boss's sheaf of newspapers. The two bodyguards, keeping fingers crossed they would not be needed and could retire to their cubicle for a glass of *tinto* and a glance at the *Espejito*, willed the chief to go through the front door. Grapnel gave his finishing-up laugh, the party made a decisive move forward and Beula slipped in behind them, crossing the reception area, creeping down the long corridor to the typing room at the end, thankful that no one had noticed. Silently hanging her jacket on the back of a chair she sat down to catch her breath.

Her colleague was hunched over the telephone. "Yes," Elna was shouting, "We're invited to Don Renardo's cocktail at 6.15. Then to Phuff's for supper. Between ourselves, I don't give a hoot whether we go there or not…All right, show our faces. Then go on to the Zonatricia…Wait for me in the public office at five forty-five. No not busy, not at the moment. Yes…I get along with her. Sweet in some ways. Competition! You must be joking. Hardly our kind I would have thought. Definitely 'Phoon for the fish knaves'…Mif would certainly sum it up…Oh, early to middle forties…No, better not. I don't think it would work…I'm changing in the office. My black, fox-trimmed."

3

"Did you see what time that new gel got back from lunch? Good God it was past three o'clock. At this rate she'll be eligible for a first warning. Now, while you're here, tell me the main thrust of your talk with the General. Just the main substantive headings."

The chief and number two stamped slowly down the corridor, pausing at every other step, the two bodyguards and chauffeur trailing behind. The party idled outside the chief's door while the newspapers were handed over. The guards and chauffeur were told to stand by, which meant a free period. Perking up, the guards retreated to their booth while the chauffeur took himself off to the Hotel Centrico's Turkish bath and massage room.

"Do you know?" said Grapnel, "You listed those points in exact order? Has anyone ever told you you have the sort of brain that finds its way to the highest levels?"

"Yes sir," Phuff replied, "My headmaster once said as much."

"What sort of age are you?"

"My age, sir?"

"I've forgotten."

"Forty-seven, sir."

"Is that all? You look as if you haven't had a decent night's rest in weeks."

"Been lying awake working out security equipment terms."

The chief looked up sharply and scanned the number two's large face, red veins at the cheekbones, sagging paunch. "Well, as regards tomorrow's meeting at the Banco, lay the case out as we've discussed. Then you'd better take a few days local leave. I don't want to see you get a return attack of hepatitis."

Grapnel thrust open the door to his suite. Charlotte, his secretary, placed the apple she was eating on the other side of her typewriter as the chief, flat headed and immaculate, strutted through her office into his, leaving both doors open. She rose, waiting to be conjured up by his agonized buzzer, but hearing sounds of settling down, pulled his door to and closed her own.

*

Beula started typing Draft Two of the Electronic Security Signals Contract for Land and Estate Protection, aka Operation Hilda, passed to her via the Poison Dwarf. A mass of scribble and balloons, it contained technical terms she could hardly read. In her numbness she typed mechanically, making no sense of the document beyond basic syntax. She did pause briefly over a phrase that looked like 'a cultivated' deciding that it must be 'a cultural' and added the word 'loan' to make sense of the paragraph.

At the bottom of the page, sheds began to appear. Whenever conflict came to the fore it came accompanied by floating outhouses, transparent yet distinct: Mrs. Bullivant's, small and neat, newly creosoted by her choleric husband; the Kettlehole shed in dull conifer green, sagging in the middle. Mrs. Brownbill's asbestos. Mrs. Waterman's kitchen extension. With these arose the urge to quit, an immense swell like a spring tide. For seconds at a time it reared up behind her swivel chair, urging her to the door. But unable to move she remained glued. The strain of want-to-leave-but-can't brought on the start of a headache.

No one in their right mind leaves a job with rent allowance, plus pension at age sixty. She had no choice but to stay put, especially now, looking early to middle forties. Especially after all the care with accent and dress to be described as Mif. Milk In First in conjunction with fish knives means low life. She is Milk in First, Early to Middle Forties. Darker visions overtook the sheds: retirement, sitting down night after night to a meal for one, reluctant to go out, afraid to come home. Tears dimmed her reading glasses, blurred the hodgepodge of script. Only when locked in the last cubicle of the Ladies could she put her head between her knees and flow with the storm, quieting sobs with squeezed out toilet paper. As Elna's evaluation circuited her brain, the orgy of grief intensified, moving towards its climax.

*

"La cosa es este," said the Senior Trade Delegate to General Tazul, "By taking advantage of today's price and avoiding the April 5 increase…What's that?" He bent down and absently picked up a paper clip, "Quality did you say? Planned obsolescence! Well there are foreign components but very few. I'll get you an updated version of the draft."

Laying the telephone down Grapnel pressed one button, then slammed another long and hard. He drummed on the leather desktop, then relaxed his hands, sitting in reptilian stillness, eyes twice magnified by the bi-focals, alert and poised for eruption. Reflecting on staff incompetence, the pink of his brow began to deepen. He swung his chair round to face the window, reversed it to face his washroom door, then turned it to the conference table, knitting his facial muscles in introspection until, rattling the middle drawer of the desk, he drew out a humidor. Setting it on his knee he snapped it open, and meditated on the contents, selected a smoke, sniffing both ends and replacing it, removed another and replaced that, took out a third.

*

Beula felt the horror start to crumble when a contradictory message whispered, "You're not in your forties. Not any age. Not any class." Her breathing slowed. Why would they even be discussing me? After all, when Elna turned round she didn't give a start or try to explain. Said something friendly like, did I have a good lunch? She rose from the toilet, gave her arms and neck a good stretch and examined the damage. As if in affirmation, the mirror image showed up refreshed, youthful even, purged of pain. Blotting her eyes on the roller towel, she rinsed her reading glasses under the hot water tap and put them on. It would never do to be seen with sore eyelids.

4

"Come in," the Senior Trade Delegate called out to a knock at the door, "Ah Charlotte." His secretary stood unsmiling, head on one side, hands clasped in an almost motherly pose. An admiral's daughter, he thought. A decent public school education. He'd heard of her father even.

"Haven't I asked you not to leave your office without a word?" Grapnel stared at her pale skin with bluish tints, ultra-fine coppery hair, light gray eyes. Youth has a blown-up look, the chief concluded. Pumped up cheeks, pumped up chin, pumped up rear.

She jutted her chin forward, saying in a kind voice, "What seems to be the difficulty?"

He thumped the desk. "Were you on the other line?"

"No."

"In the Ladies?"

She remained in the same pose with feigned civility.

"Is Draft Two complete?"

"Not yet."

"Tell Elna to come in."

"Elna's sending a telex."

"Then get that new girl," he made a shoving gesture of dismissal. Taking a cigar clipper out of a tin chest, he snipped the end of a smoke, placed it between his teeth and concentrated on lighting it, waggling the cigar around. Three matches did the trick and after a bout of coughing he drew on it in somber pleasure. Amid belches of blue smoke, he re-read Draft Two.

The door burst open and Jeremy Jooning, the number three, crossed the carpet and pulled up an armchair. A minute passed before the number one looked up.

"Put your head out of the door and tell the floozies to keep interruptions at bay for fifteen minutes."

"I wonder if I might open the window?"

"The draft blows my papers about."

The light filtering through the venetian blinds played on Jooning's jet black hair. Sometimes he looks particularly foreign for an Englishman, the chief thought. Where would he get a nose like that? Well, his people come from Blackpool.

The door opened silently and Beula was crossing the carpet with the slow controlled tread of the mannequin.

"Ah," Grapnel managed a glad smile, "Beula Kettlehole. I didn't see you at the New Year's Eve dance did I? No, couldn't have done." Both men were taking notes on her looks and manner. The chief took in her bleached hair and green eye makeup. Jooning tried not to stare. Looking away, he made a mental picture of her mini-dress and matching mesh tights.

Beula sat at one corner of the immense desk pencil at the ready, as the men turned their attention to Draft Two. "Double spacing," said Grapnel and, as Beula began to scribble, pressed the intercom, "Juan, I don't see my cigarette lighter. Did I leave it in your office por caso? I'm sending a girl over to collect it or a box of matches." As the door closed he noticed book matches on the desk and after one or two attempts, took a giant drag from the cigar, holding it some distance from his face, smoke curling in peaceable eddies, blending into the funnel of sunlight from a gap in the window blind.

"Let's talk about the interest rate," Grapnel took a suck from the cigar and became intense,"The UK bank won't budge one point from ten per cent." He leaned across the desk with a serpentine stare, "Which percentage won't they budge from?"

"From ten, sir."

The chief sat back. Through the silence came the roar of the city, clatter of small trucks, hoot of taxis, thunder of heavier trucks.

"Pepe Tazul says the Latifundia Fraternity will only pay eight," the chief balanced the cigar on the edge of the ashtray and rubbed his hands, "I don't mind admitting that electronic security is," he looked grimly coquettish, "a pet scheme of mine." He edged round the desk, "Each finca will have its own warning system. Otherwise," he sighed, "those tracts may lose their character. Scarred mountain sides, erosion. Don Fedoro's got the right idea. You were down at La Galena for the shoot?"

"I'm a terrible shot, sir."

"He has had the sense to plant banana between the coffee plants. On the other hand there are tenants who leave advocadoes on the ground."

The door squeaked and Beula was gliding across the carpet.

"Christ what are these, kitchen matches? Take them back to Juan Minuto with my compliments. No, as you were. Take them when I've finished this dictation."

Beula stood for a second or two, uncertain and forlorn, holding her gold neck chain, then nodding mechanically she apologized, drew herself upright, and with great care sat down.

Grapnel relit the cigar.

"Where was I?"

"Avocadoes on the ground, sir."

"They don't seem to know about diet. It's like Shakespeare's day when peasants lived on ale and bread, except here they don't know how to brew ale. But they do know about stealing harvested crops."

The telephone gave a piercing ring. The chief put the receiver to his ear and the ringing continued. "Pepe," he flapped an arm, whispering, "All right Jooning you can go," to Beula, "Not you. Yes Pepe, yes my dear fellow. You can tell me. There's nobody here but a secretary. You're still not convencido? The stuff is of UK fabrication. One or two components from the U.S. That doesn't mean the whole system will fall apart."

*T*he following afternoon, Beula, having reached the foot of page 18 of Draft Three, stared at a mass of indecipherable script. She jumped when Charlotte put a hand on her shoulder, asking if she'd be a sweetie and take in the number two's afternoon tea, for which Luisito is warming the pot.

Beula rose, glad of a break, "Make sure it's poured into the Doulton cup," Charlotte added, "Green china with gold edge. Camber gets the first cup which shouldn't be strong. Few drops of milk which must be today's."

"Yes," replied Beula, "And I'll be sure to see they're put in last."

Charlotte thought for a moment then added, "Sugar. One level teaspoon," wrinkling her eyes in an automatic smile.

Beula plodded down the corridor to the guards' cubby, shoulders drooping. In their glass cubicle both bodyguards were studying football pools. Luisito, the day porter, building a dollshouse out of matchsticks, looked up from gluing with vexation as Beula repeated Charlotte's instructions. With one bright eye and one half-closed, he indicated by a wag of the head that he did not need to be told what he knew. The kettle was on the boil three minutes ago. The two minutes needed for transit and one for pouring added to the correct six-minute brew. He lifted the glass tray over the chimney of the dollshouse, handed it over and limped ahead to open the door of the Assistant Trade Delegate's office. Phuff was nowhere to be seen. Uncertain of what to do, Beula saw Jooning peering through the glass partition. Timidly she looked about for a place to rest the tray.

"Let me relieve you of that," Jooning called out, stepping out of his cubicle, "Camber isn't back yet. I was wondering how much longer I could hold out. Didn't I see you yesterday? I don't believe we've met. Jeremy Jooning."

She smiled cautiously, "Beula Kettlehole. How do you do?" He returned her smile wearily, took the tray and set it on his desk, "I must have been in hospital when you arrived."

"I believe you were," she said with genuine concern.

"Kidney stone. The whole exercise almost did me in."

"How do you get something like that?"

"Some American I met down in the llanos told me not to drink the…"

Beula, watching his mouth and greenish eyes, found she had missed what he was saying.

"It only goes to show," he wound up, "that you should never ever put that stuff in your drinking flask. When did you get here?"

"It's…it's five weeks yesterday."

"Kettlehole," he mused, "that's an odd sort of name."

"What about Jooning. Th-that's pretty odd."

"We Joonings go back to the Vikings."

"We Kettleholes go back to the Ice Age."

He raised Phuff's teacup and looked over the top with something akin to interest, "And how shall you like it here Ms. Kettlehole?"

"It's like, it's well…surreal."

"Yes," Jeremy stretched, squeezing his eyes shut, "As a matter of fact that sums it up. Here things get enigmatic. The other night we escaped to the local revival house to see Lawrence of Arabia. I do so enjoy the epic style of…"

As he talked Beula noted that in a slightly seedy way he was handsome. His teeth were not good and he took care not to show them but his olive pallor combined with a nearly black suit might in recent past have aroused her interest, made her afraid of letting it show. But he's married, she thought, starting to unwind.

"It was all posted up outside. Bedouins and horses. By the time we got seated it had started and I wondered what Deborah Kerr was doing in the oasis. Until I saw Yul Brynner. To complicate matters the manager didn't know what I was talking about. When I took him outside to verify, all the signs had been replaced!" His face crumpled. "So yes surreal it is. I'm compiling an alphabet of local impediments. We're at F. Fleas, Fumes and Flatulence. What do you think? Omnipresent, partly-combusted and balls of cotton."

Beula frowned then started to laugh, "What will you do for G? What about Gratings, Grayness and Gringoes?"

"Not bad, Beula, not bad. I think we have to fit Gob in somewhere. Splattered all over the curb. Yes, that's it. Gratings, Gringoes and Green Gob. I say, where have you been hiding yourself? I'm going to call you Beuly. How is it I haven't seen you at parties? Didn't Camber give the usual newcomers cocktail?"

Beula glanced at her nails, "They combined farewell drinks for my predecessor with a welcome for me." She wasn't going to let on that at dinner afterwards, the whole group, except for filling her wineglass, had made her feel like wallpaper.

Watching her, he got subliminal messages about hairdressers, isolation, deprivation. He turned away to face the window looking down to a row of night spots catering to daytime clients. His stomach was settling down. He put the teacup back on the tray. "Look here, Beuly, Rowena and I are having a buffet supper this coming Thursday in honor of her father's sixtieth birthday. We're composing a joint telegram to send to the old boy. Try to make it. Round about eight. Informal."

Beula frowned, remembered she was frowning and tucked a strand of hair behind her ears, "I'm...I'm on call this Thursday."

"Give them our phone number. Ah Elna. The rest of Draft Three's on my desk." Elna in navy and white gingham, smiled prettily, giving off some paralyzing emanation. Jooning threw an arm around Elna and whispered into her bushy hair, "Now I want you to take Beula under your wing. Camber's having a blowout tomorrow night for Don Fedoro and the LatFrat so be a duck and see if you can wangle her an invite."

Elna's smile remained fixed. She had a busy manner even when still, "Will try. But you know we're under a mountain of paper with all these drafts." In a rush of petticoat and 'Shalimar,' she went stomping down the corridor.

"It's kind of you," Beula began, jittery from Elna's mock-friendly eyes,

"I've got another idea. Your predecessor broke the heart of a friend of ours, John Verkoke. Here's his number. Tell him I told you to suggest a drink at the Salvador. He's lost about a stone and bought himself a motor bike." Pulling open the door his manner switched, smile fading into something like petulance, "Give this back to Luisito and tell him to bring the number two's tea as soon as he appears, and that it should be medium weak with very little milk."

*

On return from the Banco meeting, Camber Phuff stumped across the reception area and down the corridor to his department. Outwardly calm, he asked himself what aberration would induce Grapnel to bypass him to brief a number three—Jooning of all people. The chief must be getting off balance. Only last week he was berating Jooning's lack of flair. That's on the mark, thought Phuff, Jooning's about as lustrous as an uncut lump of emerald and as valuable. Can't extract headings from narrative. Can't even line up events in sequence. Trouble with subordinates is, they will essay the leapfrog. Jooning must have caught Grapnel in a weak moment. I wonder if the trigger wasn't that visit by the international insurance rep? Coverage plan excluding any reference to abduction. Grapnel standing for fully a minute. Me having to hustle Dr. Braganza off the premises. There's logic in his position, Phuff allowed, poor beggar feels the more precautions the more likely he is to be knocked off. Won't hear words like shanghai or restitution. Now talks of riding in a red Mercedes! Phuff reached in his InTray, marked out one file to Juan Minuto. The one thing Grapnel won't do is take a taxi. Perhaps he'd like to try a motor bus! Phuff sniggered. Imagine the *cacique* seeing a seat vacated and waiting a decent interval for the pathogens to scatter! In a Savile Row suit!

Phuff sipping from the teacup, endured the bitter taste of old tea doctored with water off the boil. Wasn't the blonde typist supposed to have attended to that?

6

*E*very afternoon, once she had returned from the market, finished lunch and washed the kitchen floor, Nolita the maid would go to the closet, take out a witch's broom, dustpan, and feather duster. With cheerful ferocity, she'd gather Beula's three books and place them on the bookshelf, with the Spanish title on top. Blaring radio was the signal for Remedios the portera to tap on the door and look in for a few minutes. Her immodest laugh would ring out as they covered the chairs and carpet with copies of *El Espejito.*

"*Ay que lindo piso,*" the portera cried for the hundredth time, "It would be suiting Remedios down to the ground. What she has for a sitting room alone is five times the size of our whole living space."

Nolita spread newspaper on the sofa seats, on the arms and on the floor in front of the sofa. "It beats me how you lot fit into that black little hovel of yours. No bigger than the *dueno*'s saloon car. I can't picture you all getting to sleep. Piled up on top of each other like firewood? What were those last two kids doing staying the night? You said they were up and away."

Remedios sank down among the papers, "They only come of a Sunday or else when my husband's away on a job."

"Job! *Carambas*, what can he do? Did he put up my notice for the tenants, the one about doublelocking the garage? He couldn't even hold the screwdriver. That job was left to Nolita which I had to do standing on a chair. When are you going to ditch him? You're young enough to get off the hook if you hurry."

The portera roused herself, trod the newspapers then swung around, hands on hips under the poncho, "I'm young enough, yes," wagging her head, "And I used to be thought of as easy on the eyes. But how can I? He couldn't kill me. He's got no muscle. But he might get a friend to trip me up."

"Where would he find pesos?"

Remedios scanned her profile, standing on tiptoe to look into the mirror, cocking her head to see her nose from the side.

"*Bueno*, the best thing is wait for him to croak because by the look of him it may be next week. He looks sicker than death itself. And the smell! Not like a man who works all day in a mine or even a drain. That's new dirt."

The portera held up a hand, "Please! We are speaking of the senorita. I maintain she is fortunate."

"You don't have to be a gipsy to know that. She's super-fortunate. Although this living room isn't much larger than Nolita's own room."

"But your room, where is it? In the thirty-third. Nobody with any savvy wants to live over there. How many buses do you have to take? She has all this space. In this *barrio* Here in the eighth with the nobs. Two bathrooms, beautiful clothes ay and all her teeth."

"I have all mine," Nolita opened wide and made a circle with her head, "All I do is stay away from the dentist and eat a raw onion every Friday night. And don't tell me what I know about this neighborhood. I was slaving for Doña Clara before you were born. The point is, if you haven't grasped it, the senorita doesn't see her good fortune. It all comes down to loneliness and el amor. Remember el amor ?

Remedios puckered her lips, "After the first child I knew it was a fraud."

"The senorita thinks if she can find the Man all will be well. In the meantime she has a bleeding heart. She gives me a half-day off every Friday in exchange for an extra three or four hours of a Saturday morning." Nolita arms folded, stood back to the window raising herself to her full height of almost five feet. "The senorita has no one but me. She won't get any change out of those delegation people. Still she doesn't backbite. Mainly bcause she doesn't know them as I know them." Nolita stumped into the kitchen and returning with Beula's peacock blue coffee pot, poured out two glasses of espresso, sugared one, handed it to Remedios and put the other with a coaster on the sideboard.

"This week has been an unblessed one for the senorita. She told me it started up like a firework then broke into splinters and sank into—what did she call it? Some twaddle like: 'I-can't-and-even-if-I-could-who-would-let-me?' Now she's saying, 'Nobody gives a damn.' That's dead right but I didn't let on. *Mira* why would any of that crew bother with her just because she cosies up? They see and Nolita sees what they see. She won't get a come-on from any of them, not the ginger-headed miss, not the dwarf not the aging Romeo. Least of all from His Excellency." She spat on a rag and rubbed a spot on the sideboard, "On a weekday in those silly little shoes she hobbles all the way up to the funicular. Sees the cable car sliding up the mountain and thinks the view will fix everything. I bet she was panting by the time she got to the ticket office and saw Jesus Jimenez."

"The one who married Paquito's widow? Works at the funicular?"

"Sits there. Tells the senorita in his left-handed way they only sell blanket tickets to tourist guides. And on a weekday, unless you want to send that husband of yours up there, the routine is, you take a rifle and at the top you fire three shots in the air!" Nolita's face cracked, deepening her wrinkles, lighting her up from within. "Look, I do what I can. I tell her, Drive down to the hot country to that hacienda. I say, Borrow a paso horse and go riding in the coffee groves. She went once, didn't speak to a soul. By the time she got back she was more depressed than if she'd been sitting here with the radio. Ay, with her chances I'd tear the world apart."

"There must be something wrong with her."

"There's something wrong all right. Must think she's missed the boat."

"No," the portera on her bed of newspapers, spat, "She caught the boat and I'm the one on the shore. That little trip up to the coast over Christmas! I bet it was your idea."

Nolita hooted, "My idea! Never. She'd only just arrived. She needed my company. Begged me."

"Don't hand me that line. You were dying to go."

"*Que si, que si,*" Nolita cried, whooping like an eight-year old, "*'Quisiera ir,*' I told her. 'I want to go.' Wouldn't you? Do you think I could sleep that night? On the way to work I went to the Iglesia de la Virgin de Monserrate and prayed to San Isidro that she wouldn't change her mind."

"You'd never been before, had you?"

"Well, have you?"

"In my dreams."

Nolita gazed across the mill-race, beyond Doña Clara's fence, "Ay, those days by the sea! Nolita all morning on the warm sand, feeling the sun on her knees, on her bunion. In the elasticated bathing suit of Doña Magdalena, the aunt of the president before last. Ay, evenings in restaurants just the two of us. Everything paid for including my wages." Raising eyebrows, she gave a knowing nod, "Cocktails with the stationmaster while the senorita got dressed. Chicha, potato chips and aji," she slapped her thighs, "He invited me."

"I suppose the local men were following you around and not her."

"Men!" more whooping, "Is that what they are? It is strange though," she wiped an eye, "Everywhere I saw glances. But not one *piropo*, not one *buenos dias.*" She had a cloud around her, a sort of silence that was, yes, gloomy. That was her silence. Not mine. To me, nearly fifty years old, that trip, my one and only visit to the seaside made me think how a bird must feel leaving the cage, stretching its wings, feeling them beat against the air. I felt myself rising. Ay, those evenings walking back to the Hotel del Mar, knowing I wouldn't have to cook, sitting in the Bar Mirador drinking whisky! Ay."

Nolita drained the coffee pot, holding tight to the lid, "She took with her five outfits—one for every single day. Such colors: orange, gold, bluish green, all *linda linda.* I know and I don't want this to go any further, that she went up there to find not just a man but Amor. From the start I knew it was doomed but the last thing I do is forecast disappointment. Besides, miracles do happen, thanks be to the Blessed Virgin. There could have been, up there on the coast, wedged in between the fishermen and the students of *burrologia* some *hidalgo* or other, even a swell at our hotel. But you have to ask yourself what would he be doing there? She came right out with it in the middle of the night with the train bouncing all over the place. I practically had to stand on my head to hear. She said that far from attracting notice, she hadn't even met with ordinary things like smiles and kindness. She there sat wiping her eyes and blowing her nose until the breakfast cart came round. I thought it was never coming and I was more than ready for my *arepa con uevo.* I had two as a matter of fact with my beer. And even after I'd got the hot milk for her coffee—she wouldn't have a breakfast roll so I had hers—she was still snivelling. I tried to explain that as far as the trip was concerned she had luck on her side not getting in with the walking cases hanging round the hotel. She didn't say one word for sixteen hours. *Pobrecita.*"

7

*E*ating from a tray on her lap, Beula found herself pondering the virtues of diffidence. At secondary school Mr. Shearwater had kept her in to write hundreds of times "I must not talk." There was Cecil Dallant's look following her undigested opinion on what makes a genius. Short, terse statements were more or less okay but once into explanations Cecil would start up, "Braying, Beula, braying." The specter of the frozen smile at the evening's end and "I'll-ring-you," forced her to sit out the answer to a question and keep her own answers short. Of course her mother could string together eight or nine sentences. But she didn't count. Beula had learned to parry shots like what does father do? Just recently she'd been able to say he was dead.

She smoothed her blonde hair, retouched, twisted and coiled by Don Orlando whose elegant, humming salon abetted current notions of beauty. Under the rosy incandescence, Beula's head was tipped this way and that to ensure appeal from the nape of the neck, behind the ears, from the crown. Mentally she began to prepare herself for Jooning's friend Verkoke. On the telephone he'd sounded game. She took the dinner tray to the draining board for Nolita, and switched on the coffeemaker. As she poured Remy Martin into a balloon glass anxiety began to resound.

Despite adherence to the ground rules what had she got to show? In not one of her numerous affiliations had any hint of binding commitment not been scrupulously avoided. She'd met with curious kindness, but any reasonable prospect had the connections lined up. Sprawled in front of the window boxes, she poured coffee. Going on seven o'clock, dark enough for her forlorn reflection to manifest. Topknot white under the center lights flooding forehead and nose, leaving the eyes in two cushions of shadow. With a sigh she unwound her hair, sending it in a cascade around her waist as she checked every window lock, while dwelling on the fact of delegation people going home to families or spouses, of Elna and Charlotte having each other, of her fear of the streets at night and her nerviness about staying in.

She sipped from the demitasse. The main obstacle was the itinerant nature of the job. No sooner does she land at a new capital, put out feelers, than the order comes to pack and translate, eventually to pop up in another hemisphere with a similar cast of characters. Now in the high Andes at eighty-six hundred feet, the envy of her married friends, on the thirty-seventh night of solitude, excepting Christmas at Santa Marta with Nolita, she was marooned. Rising from the sofa she leant over the window-box to sniff the sweet william, squinted across floodlit stretches of parkland and urban villas and back to the pendula beech tree, little grass quadrant, moon-shaped geranium beds, watching for a sign of life, a maidservant scurrying to the evening shift, a delivery bicycle, the black-eared fruit bat.

8

$\mathcal{T}$he waiter pranced over and swung round a tray with two bottles of dark Mexican beer, stemmed glasses, plate of endives, basket of empanadas and two fluffy napkins. Phuff was spelling out that if Operation Hilda went through there could be promotion in it for the whole section. They had got to Doña Leonora's early but already the place was swelling with the lunch trade: suave men with oiled hair, swarthy men, ferocious men, all in dark suits, plus one or two assignations losing themselves in the throng. Jeremy sat well back in the booth sorting out the concept Blanket Promotion. "What I see is this," he lay emphasis as one slightly the worse for drink, "Promotion for Grapnel yes but for the rest of us an MBE—my own bloody efforts or in your case perhaps an OBE—Other Buggers' Efforts."

"No Jeremy, the chief has stated, and this is for our ears alone, Operation Hilda automatically leads to promotion. That means me and you."

"What about people like Juan Minuto?"

"That's tricky because he's on the supernumerary maximum. I say, these empanadas get better all the time."

Jeremy took an empanada and stick of endive and lay them on his plate, "You know that at this altitude, one's best can't be what it could be."

"On the other hand," Phuff said carefully, "A breakdown of the transaction might result in staff restructure."

Jeremy chewing slowly, paused and unhooked from his mouth what looked like a toenail and laid it on the side of his plate.

"Didn't I see the latest Trade Office Directive buried somewhere on your desk?"

"Had trouble catching on," Jeremy mumbled, "Storyline out of focus."

Phuff rubbed his moustaches, "It clearly states that fifty per cent of staff of certain posts like ours may be restructured if this year's trade figures fall below the sixty million mark."

"What sort of restructure?"

"The short answer is they get the boot."

A dazed Jeremy moved his elbow as a madonna-of-the-rocks came to clear away dishes. He looked under her arms as she flicked crumbs across the tablecloth onto the floor. Standing just inside the door a large woman was singing in a loud and thrilling contralto. Silence had fallen between them coinciding with the end of the song and the rattle of coins in a cooking pot, "We're nowhere near the sixty million," said Phuff after a lull.

In a rush of nausea Jeremy looked around for something to deflect it, saying, "What do you think of that new girl?"

"Which one?"

"The blonde typist."

"Girl!" Phuff rolled his eyes, pushing out his lower teeth and rocking his head. "Got all the stops pulled out."

Jeremy sneezed, "Puts me in mind of a cake. Pink and white icing. Sugar sprinkles. An herbaceous border with selvias and tulips and cineraria with hollyhocks and peonies and…"

"Ranunculus."

Jeremy stretched and started to feel better, "I suppose a certain sort of bee might want to pollinate that but it's an awfully flashy-looking flower. What price the orange nail varnish and the green eye shadow?"

"The colors don't bother me. There's just too much of everything."

"God knows what Hot Flash must think." Jeremy bit into an empanada, "By the way, has Fleur had the treatment?"

"I hope so. She desperately needed to get down to sea-level. As I do. So I'm taking a a few days local leave this weekend. A la orden senora. Muchas gracias por la cancion."

It was only when they were making their way along the Carrera that Jeremy stopped, "Wasn't Axel supposed to be joining us for coffee?"

Phuff turned to him with something like amusement, "Is it my place to give you news?"

"News?" Jeremy, pulling up sharp, attracted the attentions of a dealer in secondhand combs, "Of Axel? Is he all right?"

Phuff drew a finger across his throat, "Being flown home in the baggage compartment. You didn't look up to hearing it over lunch. No gracias, I don't want a comb because I've already got one."

"Only last Saturday I saw him down at Octavio's. At the croquet game."

"Axel had a quantity of stuff for sale. He was taken care of by two men in three-piece suits. In his own apartment. And," Phuff put a hand on Jeremy's shoulder, "They drove a car with diplomatic numberplates."

"He played off my ball most of the second half," Jeremy muttered, watching the number two stump over to the car and have a word with the yellow-faced chauffeur, Mariano, "I wanted to take a swing at him." Jeremy put a trembling hand to his temple trying to decide whether he should have a chaser. From inside a little brown bar, strains of cumbia floated his way: 'My Brother's Wake,' a pert melody, drole and *bailable*.

9

Marking the fiftieth night of solitude Beula, halfway through supper, got up to select from her albums something to rekindle the past. Returning to a tray of colcannon and beet salad, she poured out a third glass of Entre Deux Mers and looked under her eyelids at a gentleman of consequence bending from the waist. With an air of resignation she rose and moved towards the center of the carpet, lifted her arms and, putting weight on her left foot, swayed this way and that before clicking her heels. Looking haughtily over her shoulder, she stepped around the dream partner, closing with him at the hip. Between the main course and cheese she often tangoed for minutes at a time. Her partner having evaporated, she was now back in Tangier, the morning the dentist made a U turn and followed her to work, pleading with her not to go in; the twelve robed messengers, in a cluster of fezes, surrounding the gatehouse.

Night on the altiplano fell swiftly and mysteriously somewhere around six fifteen. She stared beyond the clarkia and sweet william, uncertain about drawing the curtains because then there seemed nothing left. She took the bookmark out of *Niebla* and threw herself on the sofa.

At about nine the telephone rang, silvery tones asking "*Quien habla?*"

"*Soy Beula.*"

"What's the address of this number?"

Holding her head, she banged the telephone down, muttering, Griz. Griz. Must contact Griz. She dragged up the five stairs to the bedroom, threw on a ruana and tore out to the garage. Soon she was speeding down the autopista, headlights full on and in no time, drew up at the delegation carpark.

After repeated rings Alf Hapkin, the night porter, began unlocking the delegation door, at length opening to the extent of the safety catch. As he swayed back and forth waiting for her to pass she noticed a C-shaped scab over one eye. After relocking and rebolting the door, he dragged himself over to a camp bed, holding his head.

"Are you all right, Mr. Hapkin," she called. "Could I make you some tea?"

"I'm getting a rubdown with brickdust and oil," he replied, patting the scab with a dishcloth.

"I could look out the first aid box."

"No," he rested on the camp bed rubbing his face, "because anything I say will be taken down and altered and used in my favor against me."

"*Dear Grizelda:*

What with pressure at the office and the strangeness of this city, I some-times stretch out after work and wake up at three fully dressed. Nobody goes out on foot after dark. I see neighbors rolling out of their gates. There's nothing to stop me driving around as I'm doing tonight. The only people in sight are police and soldiers.

The invitation to Camber Phuff's buffet for the Latifundia Fraternity never appeared. By the time I'd got up nerve enough to ask the Poison Dwarf what time it starts, I overhear them talking about 'last night.'

Jeremy Jooning's party to compose a singing telegram to his father-in-law was put off.

I get to the Salvador five minutes late and no Verkoke. I order a Tom Collins, finish it and get the check before he shows. He talks of nothing but the valve springs of his new motor bike and why local women stuff themselves on yucca. I might as well face it, he showed up as a favor to Jooning. Halfway through the evening my stutter turned on.

At least the secretaries' banquet came off at Dimitri's. Women women women draped over barstools, perched on davenports. Waiters in gray and white livery. Any cocktail, any kind of hors d'oeuvre from repulsive looking trout with currants for eyes to stewed breadfruit. All to songs about love on the paramo. I got curious about the bill and the two women next to me laughed in a deep-throated way & told me their jefe was hosting & could not be there. He's of the first family, known to his intimates as Don Fedoro. Naturally they were not his intimates.

At the memorial service for Axel Something, a Swedish #3, I'm wedged between two delegation wives who said to get in the swim you need a friend and in order to make a friend here you already have to have one. I can't very well admit to isolation from Saturday afternoon to Monday morning so I work through the coffee break because I'm sick and tired of hearing who drove who to the Zonatricia Bar at 3AM.

I might as well face the facts. Time has started to run out."

In the deadnesss of the office, the night porter's song rang out, "Give me your Charlie Ryall…"

10

*J*eremy Jooning felt his stomach nose dive as he crossed the Carrera against the winking amber lights and made his way through honking taxis assembled from wrecked cars. From his calculations he was between seven and ten minutes late, acceptable taking into account a lack of public clocks and hazards of wearing a wristwatch. Time's mysterious, he decided, ducking a beggar making a beeline for him. In Algiers Time didn't exist. Here in America del Sur it wasn't as if Things Take As Long As They Take as they predictably do at home. And there's a variant on Time is Money because delay also means money. On the altiplano the norm is to arrive late.

His lunch with Don Fedoro re Operation Hilda had been achieved after seven phone calls, three messages and two changes of plan. If Hot Flash hadn't summoned him he might have been over-early. The conversation began to play itself over, cacique calm, tone reasonable, ghost of a smile.

"All right, Jeremy, what is it you must do in regard to the two per cent gap? I assume you know what I'm alluding to. Well now, what am I alluding to?"

"Sir, the discrepancy between the eight the LatFrat want and the ten the UK bank wants."

"Good. Now in negotiation..." Jeremy's recall became less clear until the clap of thunder that had marked Jeremy's suggestion of nine per cent.

"I'm sorry but did I hear...Eleven was it? Sir, I'm at a loss. Don't feel it to be appr...Will try to...to..."

*

At the Hunt Club Jeremy stood on tiptoe to peer through the goddess Hestia's navel engraved on the frosted glass of the Saloon door, at Don Fedoro, long-haired and unanxious, in a pearl gray suit, spread over a Louis XIV velour bench. As there was no knowing how long he'd been there, the only way to treat it was *allargando*. As Jeremy crossed into his line of vision the grandee rose thumb in waistcoat pocket and balancing himself like a brown bear advanced for the *abrazo*. Holding Jeremy close with one arm, he grinned, "Ah, Senor Jooning, I remember you. What a miracle it is to see you in Senor Phuff's absence. You are a little wan. Let's sit at the bar for a moment and stretch our vertebrae." Jeremy noted a very definite churning of the intestine as they sat at the bar, content to suspend their common purpose, Don Fedoro's smile broadening, "The amoebas might feel threatened by a little scotch, might they not?"

"Very well, scotch it has to be. And not on the rocks. That my gut can't negotiate. You fellows can take it but we plainsmen have to make it on five cylinders."

As it was bad form to come direct to the object of the meeting, they sat searching out suitable openers.

"I read the account of the shooting of the Swedish number three," said the banker.

Jeremy's color faded, "I don't mind admitting, Don Fedoro, that I haven't had a full night's sleep since." He laid out an arc of pine nuts on the arm of the bench, "Never having resolved in my own mind whether Axel's death was planned or not."

"Ah," Fedoro sipped whisky, "I've puzzled over that myself. In my view the incident was sparked off by a difference of opinion on something minor. The final price of a cassette recorder perhaps. Some little piece of petticoat."

Jeremy relaxed, "And if it were over petticoat, would you term that minor?"

Fedoro chuckled, "Minor only to some! One tragedy in my own family was over a woman that looked very like that new blonde at your delegation." His smile faded as he rose gracefully at the major domo's bidding and waited for Jeremy to precede him under the portico. The gilt and verdigris dining room was crowded with dignified hidalgos with lustrous eyes and long antique faces, with a few young women like tiger lilies, dotted here and there.

"Perhaps," Fedoro continued, "You can tell me something about her."

"Who?"

"Your office *rubia*."

"I don't know what I can tell you."

"What kind of woman is she?"

"In what sense?"

"What class of woman?"

"I suppose you could say middle class."

"What I'm coming to is she, could we say, available?"

"I can't answer that one."

"She resembles the blonde my cousin Maximo lost his mind over a few years ago. There's something about your office rubia that reminds me of a phrase he used to describe his passion. How was it now? Yes, the *ultima experiencia*." Again the friendly smile, "You know you really should try Doña Sofia's establishment. I can recommend you for a little yellow-haired number. I'd gladly put a word in with Doña Sofia if you'd bear me in mind for the office rubia." Fedoro's eyes had become shadowy.

Jeremy stared at the menu without reading it, "I never heard of the ultima experiencia. And I don't know the lady." He lifted the whisky glass and drank with thirst, "I've been too preoccupied with Axel's death and the threat to threes in general. I'm wondering if survival lies in knowing the buyers of—equipment. Talking of equipment, how does the LatFrat view Operation Hilda?"

"Indeed we're cautious about it," Fedoro said sulkily, "It's hardly a bargain."

Silence fell as they began to cut and spear hearts of palm and push them around in the green sauce. Jeremy scanned the host menu saying, "All I can manage is a piece of haddock. Probably dates from the Ice Age," An image of the office rubia in an aqua see-through robe picked her way down a melting glacier. Pushing the menu aside, he said, "What we had in mind was eleven per cent."

Fedoro rolled a toothpick between thumb and forefinger, "You can hardly be serious!"

They paid no attention as Alvarito slid more dishes in front of them. Jeremy lifted knife and fork with shaking hands. The buzz of conversation had become a roar, "I had hoped," he began, "we might somehow find a way to build consensus on…"

"Consensus!" One of Fedoro's eyelids had reddened, "In the same breath as a raised interest rate!"

"We weren't able to go lower than ten."

Don Fedoro wiped his face with care, thrust the napkin aside, rose and edged between the tables to the main aisle. Jeremy also rose, squeezing past tightly wedged chairs, to the main aisle where he got waylaid by the major domo. By leaving a five hundred peso note and credit card, he was able to reach the front lobby just as word had gone out to summon Fedoro's chauffeur.

Jeremy stood by the plate-glass door, "Am I to conclude that ten might…might…"

Snapping shut his briefcase, the oligarch looked past him through the goddess Hestia's recumbent form, "Our fraternity is opposed to any rate higher than eight. Eight. That at least I hope you can take in. *Si Zeno, vengo.*" The glass door was pulled open. Outside, a porter rushed ahead to the car door, thrusting Jeremy to one side.

"There's just one thing," Jeremy panted, "About the office rubia, I might be able to…"

"Senor Jooning, for your own safety never mention that to me again."

11

*O*n her way back from the Ladies, Beula could see Jeremy at the far end of the corridor walking towards her at great speed. She composed her features in an acolyte's greeting, warmth without invitation. As their eyes met he looked on her with something less than inattention, scraping past with a kind of savagery. Well, she could not dwell on that today of all days. She'd dealt with snubs of greater import. Cecil Dallant in Regent Street three months after their Far East idyll, freezing in corpse-like stiffness in a shop doorway.

The problem was that of the birthday cycling round. Awake since four, she had resolved that this year *Der Tag* was not going to beat her. For one thing it has no significance to the cosmos at large. Nevertheless, anyone curious about her age had only to sneak into Grapnel's office after hours, pull the Blue Book off the mantelpiece, look up her name in the section under Support Staff and, after the fifth drink, challenge her in a dark corner at a party. What could she do but brazen it out, claim her name had been given a wrong birth date? Pretend there was a Beula Kettering in the Trade Office not to be confused with her. The fear was not that all would discover and broadcast it, rather that one or two might look up her date of birth and bide their time. Not that earlier birthdays had been anything of a revel. The day she turned six her father sending her out to buy milk and on the way home losing the change. And the beating she got! About that time her stutter started up. There was her seventeenth birthday plea for a loan towards a course on textile design that father vetoed. Design, he'd shouted, What the bloody hell do you know about design? I've seen some of your drawings and they're terrible. You couldn't design a bus ticket. There doesn't seem to be one thing you don't make a mess of. And shall I tell you why? You don't know how things work. What do you know about different kinds of weave?. For the first time in her life she'd raised her voice, citing her brother's entry into a small exclusive college. That provoked a list of proofs of her lack of brain power and skills she could never attain. Brushing aside her undertaking to repay the loan out of wages, her father had pointed out that some dizzy dames taking care with appearance and minding their p's and q's will find themselves living it up in Mayfair while you're still typing invoices.

The day, cloudy at sunrise, turned fair. Winds driving the strato-cumulus off the Montserrate mountain peak had unveiled a violet sky, exotic, disturbing. Paths down to Avenida dos Robales were bright with fuchsia. The great thrush's call echoed across the millstream, sunlight unusually clear and sparkling, temperature steady at sixty-eight. The perfect day for a suicide.

Spared strange looks and good wishes, she had spent her birthday hard at the typewriter. Retyping Operation Hilda for the fourth time had cost her her transport. The time was getting on for six and the glorious January sun lit up one wall of the typing room. Taxis were hard to pin down. Could she face the ride home by bus, take her chances on an unnumbered vehicle driven by a wild-eyed romeo, behind a dashboard fringed like an altar, the interior smelling of sweat and yesterday's dinner, with technically ten standing passengers and when the police flag the bus down to count the straphangers, being told to crouch on the floor? Well, not today, thank you. She'd just have to wait until a taxidriver took it into his head to stop. With a sigh she removed wristwatch and earrings, locked them in the bottom drawer and drew on her velvet-lined ruana. As she placed the office keys inside the press and twisted the combination, she heard Alf Hapkin, the night porter, making the rounds. She took wallet and makeup from her handbag, placing them in a mysterious pocket. Hapkin's song came nearer:

"When there are gray skies
I don't mind the gray skies…"

Damn, she thought, they've all left. Today of all days. Well, wasn't it typical?

In his terrible voice, Hapkin went on:

"I know your worth.
You make a heaven for me
On this fun-and-mirth,
Belie-he-hieve me…"

Spotting her, he lurched forward and said with unwelcome palliness, "You're working late, miss."

"How do you find this city?" she asked in a high and nervous voice.

"W'll I bin here forty-eight years. I come here from Jo-Africa and Jimerica where I made a large fortune of quatre sous."

She stared for some seconds then said, "I'm glad your sore place is better."

"I'll prove it," he said as he trailed her across the public office, "For my number tonight, I'll wear my top hat with the rule pocket. I'll carry my double-breasted walking stick with a belt at the back." At the front door he began to jig, "Oh I won't leave now I'm sure to. I lost the train I came by." She watched the inner door slowly closing on his pouchy, twitching face.

Turning, she almost collided with the chief, accompanied by chauffeur and two bodyguards.

"I didn't," she began in embarrassment, "Didn't know you were still here. I thought..."

"That's all right," Grapnel replied in a sugar-coated tone she had not heard before, "I believe we're the last. You might like to ride with us?"

She smiled for the first time that day. At the Senior Trade Delegate looking too exclusive for the hallway, at Rosario the chauffeur, Julio plain-clothes detective and Fernando, the guard. The lift was taking its time and each man gave Beula a surreptitious once-over. The chief glanced at her mascara, the chauffeur at legs, the detective, buttocks and the guard, the nape of the neck. Eventually the chief said, "We may never get out of this building. What a thoroughly unsatisfactory land-lord Don Arturo is. I suppose he's taking yet another extended holiday in Lima." All three men smiled but nobody spoke.

"The building is earthquake-proof, I believe," Beula said, feeling pressure to make inconsequential small talk.

"Is it? Dear me, I believe it might be." The chief turned to her, rolling his eyes, "Do you know anything about building construction?"

"Oh no," she tittered, feeling all eyes on her, "But I did hear via Juan Minuto that in the tremors of '67 there was um a lateral displacement but that this building remained intact."

Had she overstepped? She looked to the three for help. The detectives glowered but Rosario spoke up, "Yes *excelencia*, I remember that day very well. The 'ole building shook. I thought we was all going to die. I clasped Senora Casparides and together we prayed."

Eventually the lift shuddered down. To Beula's surprise, Phuff, Jooning and the Poison Dwarf appeared like a showcase as the doors parted, closed and opened again. Her glance lingered on the pale and sickly-looking Jeremy.

Grapnel's poker face cracked into a faint grimace, "Been for an excursion, I see."

Numbers two and three gave weary acknowledgment and the Poison Dwarf wrinkled her eyes.

"What is the surname of the landlord again," the chief asked.

"Don't have it offhand, sir," Phuff volunteered, "But I do have the name of the sidekick who manages the building."

"What Don Arturo needs is a rear kick."

Laughter roared out in the gray cell as it stuttered down to the underground garage.

"If I weren't going straight home I'd offer Beula a lift," Camber announced.

"That's all right, Phuff, I'm taking Beula," Grapnel called over his shoulder as he led across the underground vastness to where the Bentley stood in its sizeable space. There was a hush while one guard took his place beside the chauffeur, and the chief settled himself between Beula and the other guard. Silently the vehicle rolled up the ramp, paused before breaking into the jumble of trucks and vintage cars, heading north. Again the silence weighed and once they were in traffic, became cumbrous. Beula delved into the corners of her mind for something trivial but nothing surfaced, just a surge of familiar short-falls on youth, rank, interest.

"Have you made your Easter plans?" she began, and instantly regretted sounding a personal note.

"Easter?" Grapnel roused himself as if from sleep, "I say Rosario, do look out. Here comes that pothole big enough to put a Volkswagen in, change down for God's sake. And don't forget that crater a thousand meters ahead of the stop light. New tires don't grow on trees you know." He turned an unexpected matchstick smile on Beula. With hardly a grain of warmth, more like a squint into the sun, the gesture had weight. A little of the birthday depression began to dissipate.

"I may take a few days up on the north coast. I just may. What I'd like above all is to be completely idle," He lowered his tone, "To get down to sea-level, to that hotel where the toads hop about at night, to sniff the surf, get away from parties, all the noise and smoke. What about you, Beula, have you made plans? Do you have leave entitlement.?"

"I may have a day and a half by the end of the month and I'd like to go down to the hot country."

"Do you know anyone to go with?"

"Well, no."

"Ah yes, that is a problem here." Another smile and this time the detective smiled.

As she battled with three front door keys, Beula pushed out the old unaccountable fatigue that rose from the stairs, portending another evening of tension and incarceration. She could hear the plop of the portera's mop. Remedios looked up, pushed her hair back, fished in the pocket of her apron and handed Beula a letter marked Personal. By Hand from Juan Minuto. Beula took the envelope and examined it, forgetting to thank Remedios who picked up the bucket and clanked down to the main hall. It was a telex from Griz in Aden.

Beula flew up the remaining flight. It was late when she put the message aside. She had not touched her dinner. Griz's thoughts were not easy to sort out from such detail as the cost of the new shower stall and the hot winds that had all but killed the lawn. Eventually Beula was able to extract the data concerning her own situation.

All apartment walls had to be repainted in non-yellowing white and all woodwork restained. The second bedroom to be emptied of furniture and a ping pong table installed. It seemed a bit odd especially as Beula had never played but Griz added a footnote, Hidden Implications.

All bulbs to be removed from the living-room ceiling and replaced with colored lights. Fifty invitations to a disco-type fiesta to go out to partly-known individuals. Two weeks before the festivity, word had to get round the delegation that Beula was spending Saturday night in a suite at the Country Club.

Finally, she had to find two homeless cats and take *de jure* responsibility for them, with another footnote: True beauty is attainable only from within.

12

The Senior Trade Delegate cupped a hand over the telephone, "Ah Pepe. How are things on the farm? Got a milking stool yet? Hahaha. Tell you what I rang about. Wondered if you could perhaps enlighten me on cultural loans. A cultural loan...is it usual? What's that you say? It is quite usual. Do you have a definition offhand. Sorry, it's what? A sum of money advanced to museums to replace stolen artefacts. I see, Pepe. I won't take up any more of your time. And I do thank you." The STD ticked a list and redialled.

"Get me Don Octavio and make it immediate. That you, Octavio. Thank you I'm relatively well. This is in the nature of an enquiry. In going over Draft Four of Operation Hilda, I came across the term Cultural Loan. Have you got any idea what it is? Ah...*paid over to schools to enable them to enjoy special features like a music room or stage lighting?* What I need to know is how that ties in with electronic equipment? The same principle. Aha, we're getting warm. Well, Octavio, I thank you so much."

The chief's brow lightened for an instant then clouded over.

*

Beula found herself without a spare moment. There was the repainting of the apartment. She worried that her requisition might meet with contrariety in the admin section or, assuming approval was secured, the job might get started and never finished. When the water closet broke in the ensuite bathroom, two men had extracted the pump and ballcock and disappeared. Fortunately Grapnel's plumber had come to the rescue. Beula had chosen #3 Sicilian Umber for the woodwork, even offered to find a painter and decorator. But it hadn't come to that as Phuff signed all the chits on his desk including hers without reading them so that within twenty-four hours a squad of workers in paint-splattered hats trouped in to move and drape the furniture.

Feeling herself on a magic path and having to tread with care, Beula approached the stoutest of the band for the favor of the transfer of divan, nursing chair, corner desk and carpet from the second bedroom to the boxroom next to the maid's toilet. All four men lugged the items down the stairs. Then the tallest, knelt on the shoulders of the stoutest who leapt from light fixture to light fixture replacing milky bulbs with neon colors. By the following afternoon the crew were carefully folding dropcloths and tying up rinsed brushes.

After they filed out, Beula walked round and round the living room, up the five stairs to the dining space into the hollowness of the second bedroom, feeling as if every brushstroke had been hers. The scene was set. She felt grandiose and liberal. Who or rather whom to ask to the party? She knew only a few people slightly and those she did not much like. But Griz had defined guests neither as potential allies nor opponents, but ballast.

*

"Phuff, one query. What's *your* definition of cultural loan? A sum of money granted to museums to replace stolen items? A grant paid over to install special equipment? Which is it"

Phuff through a bout of coughing said he believed it was the latter.

"What would be the source of funding?"

"Well sir, presumably the grantors."

"You're familiar with the context I take it?"

"Under little roman five."

"Tell me who the grantors are." In the lull, Grapnel added, "Get back to me as soon as you find out."

The chief wore a mask of grim absorption as he opened the file, read and shuffled, shuffled and read, tying the magenta tape in a double bow. He sat a moment or two, holding still then pressed the buzzer, a loud agonized rasp, and each extension in turn. Changing color he bent down to open the bottom drawer and dive into a packet of pitted prunes.

The intercom rang, "Ah, Jooning." Loud clop clopping came on the line, "I wonder if you know what a cultural loan is?"

"I believe it's a concession granted a student in the form of a bursary, and in certain cases payment is…"

"Spare me idiotic definitions."

Jeremy felt the pitching of the delegation craft. "You might as well come out and admit you don't know," said the captain, "And since you don't know I'm charging you to collar that information."

*

Between having invitation cards engraved, deciding who should get them, sorting out disco music, what with booking a room at the Country Club and planning her wardrobe, Beula had little time for introspection.

One thing followed another. Two black cats arrived on the doorstep that Tuesday morning, the darlings of a retired American missionary, Mrs. O'Melly, who, awaking to an intruder spreadeagled on her window sill, had suffered cardiac arrest. Mrs. O'Melly's maid, Severa, wheeled Steno and Yuri over in a laundry basket and tipped them out in the kitchen, sobbing that it was all very well for them but what about her?

Nolita, unpleased with the development which looked like extension of duty and no parallel compensation, dared not voice disapproval. The senorita badly needed company. What could she say but "Ha," pointing a finger, "Fancy a thin cat lasting ten years and the fat one only eight and a half!" Grumbling, she threw a few mushrooms in with the onions yellowing in the pan.

13

"Don Amo!" Jeremy said to the head of the cultural affairs ministry, "God bless you for ringing back…Well, offhand I just wondered, if you could give me some clue to the categories of cultural loan your department deals in…Ah…Not repayable and only available in certain cases. Let me note that down. Would there be any loans that might be repayable at interest?…Well, in amounts of let's say, two hundred million pesos…Hello?…Electronic equipment. Yes…Yes…Mmm…Mmm. Well, my dear sir, I thank you so very much. I'll await your call." Jooning lay the telephone on its side and examined his knuckles. A creak behind made him spin round to Phuff in a corner draped over a typist chair.

"Cam! Back so early?"

"My memo, if you recall, set out my return date as today," An alien light shone on Phuff's spectacles as he unravelled and dusted himself down, "Jeremy, I'm not at all sure you should have named a sum like that." Crossing the reception area, he halted and made his way back down the corridor to Grapnel's office.

The number one, thumping a file up and down, patted papers in order, "Welcome back Phuff!"

"The only thing on my agenda sir, is the number three."

Grapnel relighted his cigar.

"Jooning's been in touch with Amo Medianoche, the cultural affairs chief."

Grapnel held a fist to his face, a signal for silence, staring ahead for some seconds, "There are rumors that Medianoche was at the Swedish number three's apartment the night he was murdered and that Axel was mistaken for the Austrian drug merchant occupying the apartment above."

"I just overheard Jooning name a substantial sum to Medianoche, under the heading electronic equipment."

Grapnel gritted his teeth, then sighed, "Well let's look on the lighter side. How's his marriage standing up?"

"Rowena seems well, except for a slight case of hair loss."

The STD put his pen down, "I believe that's not unknown here. Women seem to lose first their hair then their teeth. Must be high altitude acting on hormones. Now getting back to performance, Jooning does, I grant you, have the sort of mind that darts about but my gut reaction is let the matter lie," The chief put both hands on the desktop, a sign that the meeting had ended.

14

It could have been no more than a few days after the cats' installation that something happened to Beula's appearance. Only the Saturday before last she had driven down to Tierra Caliente for a day at the swimming pool. The strain of tailing a belching motorbus round bend after bend, hesitation about passing it, anxiety about falling rocks or a sudden landslide following the seasonal rains, being buried under a fifty foot mudhill, all had created tension. Nolita could see it in her face.

But last Sunday after another trip to the hot country, Beula wore a glow that Nolita had been forced to enquire about. It appeared that after miles and miles with the gas tank pointing to Empty, Beula had prayed for a filling station. None had come forth but the fuel had held out right until she'd rolled down to the front gate with the portera on hand to help push the Mini into the garage. The senorita's eyes no longer looked bloodshot. The creases on her forelip had ironed out. There were no more shadows around her mouth.

Now that the black cats had sniffed over the apartment, found niches on the bookshelf and behind the refrigerator, now that the ping pong table was installed, Beula's sagging cheeks had righted themselves. Her blond chignon had grown larger, more lustrous. She no longer looked flashy and done up. That had yielded place to some other look, hard to define. Nolita noted the changes as they occurred and assumed that the senorita had seen a beauty specialist. What was important as far as she was concerned was the feeling around her mistress, and that had always been decent. The senorita paid on time and never supervised. Gave a thank you for simple services like warmed up coffee or a polish to her office shoes. Not that she was perfect like Mr. Lanchester who had had a vacuum cleaner sent in from Miami. Nevertheless, the minute the senorita opened the front door Nolita felt glad. Around the senorita life took on an all rightness. Continuity, lump sum at the end of the term.

Beula's spirit permeated the apartment, whether she felt happy or sad and whether she was there or not. The calm intensified the closer you got to her. Once the larger cat had discovered the empyrean of her lap, he would hover until she sat down with coffee to insinuate himself between saucer and Spanish language book. Nolita had mixed feelings towards Yuri and Steno. They didn't knock things down, being past it. Didn't even claw the upholstery. And if they did? Nolita shrugged, the furniture didn't belong to anyone. If they'd torn the orange sofa to pieces a duplicate would likely be found at the delegation warehouse at the south end of town. What did nag was that in addition to commercial feed, the cats got scraps like ends of camembert and hard-boiled egg that normally would have gone to her. Nolita never stole food from the refrigerator, never stooped to it. She had a goodish dinner at home. Rice and yucca occasionally a bit of bacon, a few green beans, fresh from the stall. But lunch depended on what she could salvage from the night before.

Nolita sighed. Things were happening and not all for the best. You couldn't tie it in exactly with the big green table or the cats but it did date from around that time. The ping-pong table hadn't been in the house five minutes before the senorita's routine went haywire. She had fed the cats, but left no instructions on what to make for dinner the next evening. Worse, she'd forgotten to leave money for shopping.

Soon after the senorita's weekend at the Quinta Country Club (bill on the mantelpiece), a youth had appeared on the verge, walking in and out of the pendula beech tree, disappearing altogether, re-emerging five minutes later. Too well-dressed to be ordered away, he'd already made deferential noises to the portera and shown elaborate courtesy when Nolita had gone down to get a closer look at him, nodding his head sideways like royalty, putting out an imperial remoteness. Not more than nineteen. Had he surfaced at the country club? Nolita wondered as she brushed one or two tufts of cat hair from the wing armchair. It didn't make sense. If he's young, rich and handsome—well almost handsome—why would be bother with her? Certainly she's been looking younger lately. Ay, but she doesn't look nineteen, Nolita thought as she waggled her buttocks to the strains of *Traigami Tu Corazon.*

Then there's this cocktail. Fifty guests. The senorita can hardly know any of them and that's just as well. Because Nolita knows them beyond the honeymoon stage. Two waiters! Catered food over and above Nolita's canapes. She must be spending all her savings and for what? Wineglasses and dinner plates were already to hand. Two Indians had brought in the silverware, each piece counted, each listed with individual replacement cost, "Put it there," Nolita told them in her mock haughty manner. On the way out the larger Indian leaving the invoice on the wooden crate, threw her a sullen look over his shoulder. After the outer door had closed, a sweet smell of sweat and old mothballs hung on the air. Cursing, Nolita went to the kitchen and shovelled some coffee beans into the grinder.

Beula was turning into a goddess. One morning her face appeared lighter. The next morning it had started to glow. A few days on, the eyes grew luminous. Next she undid her hair, letting it ebb and flow. Her mannequin walk with the bent knee and tightrope tread now gave way to a casual, swinging saunter. A new silence surrounded her, the silence of presence. And her clothes. That was another side that Nolita could not fathom. Her office wear had taken on a new crispnesss as if some phantom with a magic bodkin had made a stitch here and a tuck there to bring about harmony and airiness where only care and good tailoring had been.

From the bookshelf, Yuri the larger cat looked up from cleaning his privates and eyed Beula as, in a new blueberry velvet pant suit, she frisked back and forth in the living room, watering a plant here, straightening a picture there, checking her reticule, adjusting a drop earring. The cat gave a start, eyes blazing as the downstairs buzzer sounded loud and long. Snatching up a maroon poncho, Beula tore out of her front door. Then unlocking it she flew back in to give one final twist to the window locks. With a glance at her fingers, she gasped and dashed up the five stairs to the bathroom, reappearing with a tiny bottle. The buzzing became staccato, exasperated. Both cats jumped down and fled into the kitchen. Beula, blowing them a kiss, let herself out.

"Ah Phuff, there you are," the chief cried, "I've been ringing all over the office. Where were you?"

"Well, sir, went over the translation of Draft Five with Juan Minuto then to the copy room to look for my pen."

Grapnel let out a colt's tail of smoke. Clearing his throat, he said across a blue haze, "Sure you won't have one? Does help the digestion."

Phuff took an upright conference chair, "Don't think I will, sir, if you don't mind."

The chief's mood was not easy to read. Paler than usual, his shuffling of papers betrayed a sort of grim elation. "About the Cultural Loan. It's taken me the best part of three weeks to unravel." Mottle outlines remained faint around the jowls but tension arose from where he was sitting, "Last night, I went through Drafts One to Five of Operation Hilda," he went on, "which I see originated from your department in January. Now I wonder if you would be good enough to read this phrase from A to B."

Phuff took the typescript, looked it over with great attentiveness, then looked up.

"Out loud."

With a frown, the number two lowered spectacles and read, "'…the balance to be made over in the form of an acceptable cultural loan.' Well?"

"Well, you say! I take it you're familiar with the context?"

"Oh indeed sir. On Draft Four it occurs on page 33 and on Draft Three on page 38 but on Draft Five it's been transferred from the end of little roman two to little roman four. Do you want me to recite the Draft Five section?"

"No, just little roman four."

Phuff lifted his spectacles, "'The balance of five per cent to be made over in the form of a cultural loan acceptable to all parties.'"

"That makes some sense to you, does it?"

"Well, sir, I see it as a fraction of the whole."

"Now looking back to Draft Four, would you be good enough to read page 33, little roman two. Out loud."

"'The balance of five per cent is to be made over…'" he looked up, "but it's as I said."

"So now let's go earlier and look at Draft Two, edited by Jooning. I stayed last night until half past nine," the chief went on amiably, his brow calm, "Going over every draft in reverse order. What I uncovered was this," he carefully extracted a sheet from its spiked brass clip and placed it in front of Phuff. "Here's Draft One. Read that out from A to B."

"The balance of five per cent is to be made over in the form of *collateral*."

16

As Phuff, reddening around the ears, studied Draft One, the door pushed open. The chief looked up almost in geniality, "Ah at last, Charlotte. I was just about to tell you to write out your notice."

Charlotte in starched blouse and pleated skirt, retained the cool of the established civil servant, "I'm sorry to keep you Mr. Grapnel," she said, "I only went to collect your coffee. We mustn't get het up about details." Her bustling presence brought on irritability but did not disturb his line of thought.

"Details, Charlotte. There are some details which are given weight because although not sizeable *per se*, they may pertain to large-scale matters. In this office you will rarely be privy to a small-scale detail."

"That may be," she replied, setting down the cup, saucer and dessertspoon, all the teaspoons having disappeared, "But whether I'm able to answer your call in one minute or two minutes is just such a small-scale detail."

The STD held to the executive rule of never discussing methodology with junior staff, making a mental note for her personnel file: 'Slow on the uptake. Insubordinate when tackled.' He raised the breakfast cup to his lips.

"Don't go, Phuff. Sit down. Now, Charlotte, there's been a significant error. I want you to cast your eye over this paragraph on Draft One. Did you by any chance type it?"

Charlotte, lips compressed, took the sheet of blue draft paper, put her head on one side, looked over the text and handed it back, "It's likely that I did. Although I prefer the maxi-print," she nodded at her chief, "Better for your eyesight."

Makes uncalled for personal remarks, thought the STD. Aloud he said, "Now look over this version of Draft Two. Do you think you might have typed that?"

She gave the document finicky attention, standing up and taking the page to the window, "Absolutely not."

"How can you be sure?"

"I never split a catchword and this one's not only split but split in the wrong place. It isn't info dash rmation but informa dash shun. Furthermore I always put a comma before etcetera or before id est. At Mrs. Fanters they were always very particular about punctuation."

Garrulous and cretinous, he thought, "All right, that'll be all. Send Elna in, also Beula. And," he called out, "Don't forget to clear my tray. Chop chop."

The chief's hot spots held off as he reflected on staff incompetence. For some seconds he toyed with an unlighted cigar then resolutely balanced it on the pedestal ashtray. A welcome intestinal disturbance was beginning to surge. He obediently rose and crossed the carpet to his private washroom. "You might, Phuff, look over the Exegesis," he said, holding the door, "You can stay here and dictate any changes." With a masterful turn to the handle he pulled open the door to his facilities and, with proud upright posture, strode in.

Phuff uncrossed his legs and began to scan the document for possible snags. Only a couple of weeks and his wife would be back. It had seemed an eternity Even the chief had queried how recovery from a D. and C. could take three months. Well, if Fleur had felt weak over so long a period it seemed only natural for her to spend time recuperating at her stepmother's hotel in Tangier.

The office door opened wide to admit Beula, who crossing the room with a new swinging stride, arranged herself not on the usual hard seat at the chief's vast desk but on an armchair two or three feet away, being careful to cover her knees with the notepad. Phuff, rousing himself, took up the file, "This is a draft Exegesis Ee Ex Ee Gee Ee Ess Ay Ess. Put my initials at the top and today's date. Addressed to Sebastian Xaverel, Governor of the Metaris Bank. Double spacing, copied to…" Phuff leaning on the chief's desk caught a whiff of Beula's perfume and it temporarily blocked thought. He took a breath and started on Note A. As Beula began scribbling he became lost in an analysis of the bend behind her knee. She was not wearing purple mesh tights today but ones with a golden sheen. The woman is in fact not bad looking, he was forced to conclude, lovely almost. He stared at his notes. *The woman is lovely.* Overwhelmed by work and Fleur's incapacity he had simply not noticed.

The door to the washroom opened and the chief emerged, "False alarm," he announced to the room at large, taking up cigar and matchbook, "Well now, Camber," exhaling smoke and temporarily obscuring himself from view, "Finish the Exegesis, get it typed and passed to me. I say, Beula, what a pretty frock.?"

Beula held the hem between finger and thumb, "It's a new sort of linen. Non-wrinkle." She met his eye and the atmosphere in the room softened, felt familial.

"Ah Elna! Did you by any chance type this?"

Elna advanced, looked over Draft Two briefly and handed it back, "No I didn't. And Charlotte didn't perhaps she did," lifting a hand in the direction of Beula.

Both men winced at the use of the pronoun for the cat's mother. It wasn't as though Elna's father lived in a council flat with a mother on public assistance. Elna had been to a perfectly respectable public school.

"Cast an eye over Draft Three, Elna. Did you type that?" Elna did not take it from her chief's thrusting hand, merely nodding her head, "Parts I remember but not all. I see someone dripped coffee on it. Must have been Luisito."

In the pause Grapnel and Phuff absorbed this fresh instance of her sense of honor. Then Beula spoke not in her usual treble but in a warm decisive tone, "What seems to be the problem?"

"A new category of loan cropped up all by itself."

Beula took Draft Two and looked over the passage with care while the bosses took in her details, blonde braid, arching instep, vanilla button-through dress, shadow between second and third buttons. She felt no stab of defensive panic Why the fuss about a typo? was her only thought. Silence cancelled the thunder of heavy trucks. At length she looked up and, with level gaze at the number one said, "I don't remember this particular page offhand."

"That's all right," replied Grapnel choking on his Havana, "if you're not sure, you're not sure, that's all."

17

"But which one is the one?"

Remedios, the portera, getting cramp from leaning forward too long, lounged back on pages of *El Espejito* spread out over Beula's marigold armchair. Massaging the area of discomposure, she sat upright in the chair and put out a cup for more espresso.

"*Quien sabe?*" replied Nolita, "Who knows for sure! *Mira*, I only see the senorita—well I can't remember the last time. What's today?"

Remedios, counting on fingers back to Sunday, replied, "Friday."

"So I haven't seen her to speak to for six days. Since the party. Now she tells me not to bother coming so early," Nolita's mouth tightened.

"AYayayayayayayAY." Forgetting the cramps, the portera leaned forward and hugging her knees swayed to and fro, "I heard thumping the other night."

"Santa Maria Gesu Cristo. In this house? Never. What you heard was that car dealer on the third floor."

"Couldn't have been," said Remedios, "I didn't hear the woman shouting."

Nolita pulled at a mole on her chin, "I haven't seen any signs of an overnight stay. Or smelt garlic. The bed looks as it always looks, hardly slept in."

"Maybe they had transports on the carpet."

"The senorita has more refinement than that."

Remedios with liquid eyes looked over the top of the demitasse, "You don't know whether he was here or not?"

"Which he are you talking about?"

"I mean the fiance. I heard she was seeing a North American."

"Impossible. Where did you hear that? "

"Severa got it from Amparo."

"They must be mixing her up with that other rubia —Carlotta."

Remedios shrugged, setting the half-full cup on the paper-strewn carpet.

Nolita poured a few drops of aguardiente into her coffee, "Because if she had a North American I would be the first to know. Oh, she has had one or two visitors, but I'm not going to say they're more than acquaintances. You know how foreigners are. Take up with practically anyone but it doesn't go as far as the bedroom. That party, if you noticed, was full of fiances, cast off, reconditioned and up for grabs. Don Camber, for one, was eyeing her. He's been around three years at least. I nursed him through hepatitis, remember? But for me he could have died. Exactly the color of a Stilton cheese even to the blue veins. That young wife of his had upped and left for Europe. There was no one but Nolita to wash his pyjamas, his bedsheets, spoonfeed him, shave him. Mind you, he was generous about food. I could buy whatever I liked but that drag up the mountain just about did me in. In the end he gave me the room over the garage."

"I know which one," Remedios nodded, "Hair laid flat. Big and clumsy, glassy eyes, funny little nose."

"Somehow he found himself a younger woman. For weeks and weeks she's been absent. Getting something to lubricate her vagina."

"Where in the name of Jesus did you hear that?"

Nolita with penetrating half smile, folded her arms, a sign that she was prepared to go no further.

"Who's the *chino* that stayed behind to make a nuisance of himself? Hanging round the premises, the cheeky little brat in gray whipcord? You know who I mean, rubbery face and Chibcha hair."

"I don't know which one."

The porters broke into hearty and none too pleasant laughter, "You know that with me it won't go any further."

"Only all over the town like a runaway burro."

"The kid in the three piece suit and red necktie."

"Oh that," Nolita drew herself up to her full height, "Just poked his head out of a hole in the floor of the lowest tin shack in the last corner of the shanty town."

"*Venga, venga.*"

"He shows up with the big green table and the next day I see him lurking, yes lurking, on the other side of the mill race, one moment as clear as day, then he's hiding under the big tree. The senorita comes home early and introduces him as a friend from Ecuador. Well I know and he knows I know that he's never seen Ecuador and never will. She says he's a student and I know what he's a student of. *Burrologia.* Donkey business. Gets himself invited for a game of ping pong. Once in a blue moon hits the ball. I suppose she must find him recreational. I hear them giggling over their BLS's."

"Their what?"

Nolita put on a mock high-class Castilian, "Their brandy, lime and sodas." With contempt she looked out, past the pendula beech tree, at Doña Clara's elliptical geranium beds on lawns stretching down to Avenida Dos Robales.

"Where the chino got that suit I can't think. Maybe his rich double died and left it to him. But for all the fussing over eyebrows and shoelaces, I know he comes from the tin hut. He looks around this piddling little apartment as if he's in church. As well he might. In the very *barrio* where the bigwigs hang out.

"Looking at him all polish and smiles, I see grease on the kitchen stove, dustbins on the mud floor, one toilet for five families. Three times I spot him always in the same suit. Not English tailoring but in its way it's *regular*, wide lapels, nipped in waist, flaring trousers. Not only does he wear the same suit, this I know by the missing threads under the collar but the same blue shirt, the same red tie. I hang it up while he's prancing about trying to look athletic, all fitted out in the senorita's tee shirt and shorts," she collected up the espresso cups, "After his free shower bath—black hairs in the plughole, he stands all the way on the motorbus and once home takes off the suit, shirt and tie and places them in a drawer until the next game. But..." she stopped, "That looks just...yes, here comes the article itself. It's nearly time for me to leave and I'm damned if I'm going to let him in."

Remedios, on her feet now, took up the keys to the building, "Of course you must let him in. It does not look respectable to leave him out. I'm going down for the mail."

"The senorita's not here," Nolita told the youth in response to his formal bow and burning intention. As she did not step aside, he had to scrape past her. For several moments he stood motionless in the middle of Beula's living room, a sturdy, stubbly piece of pre-Columbian sculpture.

Visitors as a class hardly noticed Nolita. She never considered that a point against since no interest at all, although objectionable, always ranked above over-interest. The danger of over-interest could not be discounted, even if in the event of compromise Remedios was within call. But, save a cursory "*Buenos dias, que hubo?*" and "*Ma que lindo gatico,*" the visitor's attention was on the room, as he strolled round and round from the window boxes of clarkia and sweet william to the five stairs leading to the senorita's bedroom and across the avocado carpet back to the kitchen. Today's wait being open-ended, he paused at the kitchen door. Nolita, waiting like a spider, poured him a jigger of rum.

"Ay Pablito, you must feel formal about the senorita."

In the waiting period he made a circuit around the kitchen stool, comparing the shine of the kitchen floor with the shine on his shoes.

"The senorita is not young," Pablito said at length, "but I am honored to be an escort. Of all the foreign ladies I have seen she is the finest dancer. No woman can move to the cumbia like her."

Nolita poured out another two fingers of rum. He walked to the end of the kitchen table. His legs were low to the ground, but to Nolita, looking up in her penetrating way, he appeared lofty.

"What a time we had," he reported, "driving the senorita's minicar all over the road in the dark with the lights out. By the time she had found her doorkey she could not stand. She has the makings of the ultima experiencia. I hold the senorita in awe. My knees sink at the sight of this house. She might almost have done for papa but he could never aspire." Humming 'La machaca, la machaca, como pica la machaca,' Pablito sauntered out of the kitchen to address Yuri who, with a shuddering yawn, winked once or twice and rubbed his large head on the bookshelf.

A North American, Nolita thought as she put away the flick brush and broom and took out one of Mr. Lanchester's former undershirts and a tin of polish, rubbing a spot of wax into the coffee table to let the young upstart see that the business of the day was not going to be held up for him. Now that Mrs. O'Melly was gone there was no North American she knew of. Of course one part of the town was stiff with them. She had taken care to steer clear since her mother and sister, both dead, had worked for Nortes who not only paid local rates but supervised.

The front doorbell gave a loud clang. Nolita put aside the rag and made her way slowly down two flights of stairs. Standing on tiptoe. she peered through the spyhole to make out the gray worsted lapels and gingery moustache of Don Camber.

18

"I say hello Nolita," Camber Phuff looked down at his boots. "How nice to see you. Would-would the senorita be at home?"

"She's expected."

Slowly and heavily he clumped up the stairs, Nolita following at a distance. Once they reached the front door she looked him over with a remnant of pride. His color had returned although partly alcoholic. He looked reasonably well cared for, although overfed. How many times had she polished those steel spectacles, wiped that tiny nose, shaved that drooping chin? Phuff's face fell at the sight of Pablito sprawled on the Ministry's orange sofa. Sitting down heavily, he concluded the boy was a relative of Nolita's. The two men, one middle-aged and substantial, the other aware of the magnificence of his youth, took stock of each other.

They have things in common, Nolita reflected, pouring out a hock glass of madeira for one and a third jigger of rum for the other. Like the kid, the fuddy duddy always wears the same suit. But Don Camber's off-the-peg tells a truer story. Nevertheless, she placed him nearer Pablito at the lower end of the economic see-saw. Changing her mind she swallowed Pablito's rum, filled the glass with ice cubes and coca cola, and set the drinks on a tray beside a dish of hand-dipped oil-cured black olives.

The lad's a grandnephew, Camber decided. How they do grow. Avoiding Nolita's eye he took the goblet and sat sipping madeira. In repose Camber's face looked tight-lipped and grim, yet, like Beula, the feeling around him was sunny. Yuri, half dozing on the bookshelf, opened his eyes fully and flattening ears in an alligator yawn, stretched, and carefully jumped down. Tail erect, he weaved in and out of Phuff"s legs, sniffing trouser cuffs. Camber sat on the edge of the chair, legs wide apart.

Pablito stared at Phuff who, looking away, wondered why young men of underdeveloped nations carry their sexuality around as though it's on a par with survival. I mean at seventeen I hardly had it in m'mind. Too taken up with study. Pablito aware of the interest of his rival, turned on a dazzling view of himself. Phuff closed his eyes. Ideally he'd like to pay a chunk off the mortgage as well as get work started on the oriel window. Then in a few months, D.V., I'll be down at sea level. The doorbell startled both of them.

Nolita dried her hands and crossed the living room, complaining that the senorita had forgotten her keys. There was shouting outside and doors banging. Both men straightened up and put feet together. "Be careful of the top," they heard, as the door was kicked open and Remedios led in two young men carrying a package six feet high, three feet across. Nolita spread her arms out in disbelief as a magnolia tree in an elaborately carved pot was unwrapped and set down against the wall. When the disturbance surrounding the delivery had abated, the women were in the kitchen. Nolita wresting a tiny envelope from Remedios, put a finger under the flap.

"Be careful," whispered the portera, "You'll tear it."

"And if I do! She's three feet above the tarmac." Holding the card in her strong brown fist Nolita, puzzled, turned it over. "I never heard of any Givemel." She opened the door to the living room, "*Ay que linda,*

linda! Ay que guapa!" Eyes aglow, she clasped her hands and spoke to the magnolia tree, "Nothing is too good for you. Nolita will shield you from those cats."

On their way out the delivery men saluted Phuff. To cover discomfort, he fumbled for an imaginary pipe. Never in his life had he seen such a display. Blooms of this order do not arrive for birthdays, he thought.

Pablito rose, tiptoed over to the kitchen door and, closing the door carefully, said to Nolita, "Is he her husband?"

Nolita opened the oven door and, seeing the pilot light out, swore as she bent down to relight it.

"I suppose he sent her the tulips."

"I suppose he did."

"I wonder what he is doing here?"

"I wonder what you're doing here?"

"I come as usual for the ping pong."

"Well, the senorita must have forgotten because she's been invited to an official party by her boss so in your shoes I'd do a disappearing act. The senorita has more important things to do than to mess around with chinos like you."

"Is he her husband?"

"Yes."

"Then he is cuckhold," Pablito looked prim, "In the North wearing the horns is no shame, my father says. The Nortes are wedded to money. Will you oblige me with one more glass before I depart?"

Nolita made a fanning sign. Not a drop of rum, coca cola or tap water. She held the kitchen door open, propelling him across the living room and out the front door.

*

Phuff rose when he saw the vision hurrying in. His heart pounded at an unusual rate making him cover confusion with a less than

cordial smile. Beula stopped, also in confusion, "Mr. Phuff...
is...everything all right?"

"I thought I'd just pop in to..."

"Oh my God, what a beautiful...what blooms! Did you...?"

"I?"

Beula ran to the kitchen and called, "Manolita is there a card?"

"Inside," came the reply.

While Beula, breathing light and beauty into the room, read the message. Phuff dropped madeira over his trousers, "I just popped in on the
offchance that you might like a lift. I don't remember if you know where
we live."

Beula became all kindness, "I must find you a rag. The last thing I
expected was for you yourself to collect me. I can find my own way. I got
my car out." Under his scrutiny she became self-conscious and fought
putting out appeal, "I forgot to ask if your party's formal or informal."

Phuff's eyes rolled down to her ankles, "I must say you're looking
glam enough for every sort of party. If it's all due to the ping pong, I'd
better start getting into shape for a game," His eyes rested on hers. She
turned with relief to the BLS Nolita had plonked on the table and sat
sipping, giving Phuff a chance to take the weight off his feet.

"My dear, you're blooming. Like the magnolia," He leant forward,
pressing hands on knees. waiting for her to rise. As trancelike she sat
still, eventually he got up and, gathering up her poncho, held it out.

"Will it be a big party?"

"Rather small in fact."

"Ten or twelve?"

"Just two."

She paused at the front door, "Just, you mean...yourself and me?"
Her manner became solemn. His head started to pulsate. There was a
screech of brakes on the arterial road. "What had you in mind?" she said
at length.

"I got in some rather special sausages. That go well with mushrooms."

Beula made a moue, "I don't eat sausages."

"Everyone eats sausages. What is there to dislike in them?"

"I don't like pork."

"These are beef, I believe."

"I don't like blood and I don't like grease."

"I think these are mostly bread."

"If they were all bread that might not be too bad. But even so, I don't really think I can come because well it…"

"Yes?"

"…would ah get around."

"Do you know where I live?" There was a note of indignation. "My house almost sits at the foot of the talus. No one on earth sees me coming or going."

She stared at her ankles.

"My wife worries about me dining in night after night. We might even find we have interests in common. I like cooking and horticulture. I also do stamp collecting." Phuff walked over to the window, "This mountain range must be one of the most extraordinary anywhere in the world. Although they're called young mountains, to me they…" he hesitated and then continued, "they're monuments to a past that confounds the consciousness." He threw open the kitchen door, "I say Nolita, your grandchild's come back."

Nolita looked up over a forkful of black beans and yucca, "Grandchild? I had no immaculate conception. Do I look like the mother of a mother? How old do you think I am, a hundred?"

"Your nephew I mean."

Chewing, Nolita peered out at Pablito who, eyes down, paced the path beside the millstream with the air of the young master of one of the adjacent houses.

"That's no nephew of mine. I don't know where it sprang from. But I've got some idea," Nolita added under her breath. Aware she had reached uneven ground she corrected herself, "He's a friend of a friend."

"A friend of yours?"

Beula came into the kitchen, "He...and his family are from Ecuador and he comes here to practice p-ping pong."

"I must say he's dressed for some sort of sport but it doesn't look like ping pong, " Phuff strode to the front door, throwing it open with such force that one hinge came loose. Halfway down the stairs he looked up, "I wonder what you've got in common with him?" His voice echoed in the stairwell, "If you want a lift Nolita, I'll be outside."

19

*A*t six o'clock Beula sat in the typing room tapping out a letter to her mother, making the tidings as dismal as possible because anything on a cheerful note got a rabid response peppered with reminders of Beula's imprudent independence of mind, display of dubious knowledge and general futility, ending on a note of regret that Beula had never married, in her mother's words, '…no bloke coming home every night.' Beula was able to identify these admonitory missives by the particular neatness with which her mother had written the address. To ward off such a reaction, she racked her brains for setbacks and minor catastrophes. Today they were hard to pin down. There were the typos found by Mr. Phuff; the lassitude at high altitude which she no longer felt. Her missing wristwatch. A caressive clasp of her inner arm, a professional snapping off, gamine running for dear life. She hadn't thought to call out 'Stop Thief' merely hastening to make the insurance claim. That part she left out.

She signed the letter and, knowing them to be Mif, added a few crosses. After placing it in the outward mail basket she applied rouge and eyeliner. Rising to secrete her wallet in a pocket sewn to her petticoat, she became aware of Jooning standing just inside the door. Jolted, not having heard him come in, she put a hand to her chest, struggling for self-possession. Jooning stockstill, eyes chartreuse green, clutched a draft memorandum.

"No, Jeremy," she said, making her voice firm, "It will have to do for the morning." She came closer and examined his nose, wide at the extremities, short in profile, "Which ah which draft is it anyway?" she asked, "I've only…only just finished slaving over Draft Six."

"It's a problem on Draft Two," he replied in apologetic tones. Her heart stopped, "No," he added, "it's nothing. What I wanted to ask was. I was wondering if you needed a lift home?"

Beula went back to dividing up the contents of her handbag, coin purse to the right, makeup sachet and comb to the left, "That is kind," she told him, "But I already have a lift with H.E."

"With H.E. eh?" Jeremy's eyes wrinkled, "Better hang onto your bollocks."

She pretended not to hear and he went on, "I wondered if you might not be averse to joining me for a drink. On the way home."

"A drink!" She ceased brushing rouge on her cheeks and stared. "Well, it is kind of you. But I really can't because the ping pong game starts at 7.30."

He paced up and down, "Well I play ping pong. Used to be rather good, actually. Practised at Salamanca every day after class. But of course these days, poor me, I've got to be home for seven because we're expecting a call from Rowena's father in Lucerne. I don't have your latitude. Still we've got forty-five minutes give or take. Come on, let's go up the slope to Jokers Point. Have a noggin at the Blue Tile Bar."

She hesitated. He froze while she zipped up the plastic sachet, "We might," she said soberly, "But what would I tell the *cacique*?"

"Tell the bugger anything. You're going ten-pin bowling."

*

"I don't think I can ride with you this evening," she told His Excellency in the manner of you're a castoff lover, as she stopped at his office to check the out tray, "I've got one or two things to do and would rather not keep you."

"It's no inconvenience," Grapnel replied, rising to the challenge, "I'll sit here and catch up on the Financial Times. Just fetch it for me, will you? Which reminds me. There's a bottle of gin somewhere and some angostura. If you'd go and find me a glass, I'll have a livener while I'm waiting." He leant against his desk watching her open and shut drawers, put papers into the press and stack files for the registry. Alf Hapkin's voice welled up in the corridor, "Give me your Charlie Ryall…"

Hapkin was leaning on the counter, hands clasped, when Beula came out of the kitchen. His toupee was the wrong shade of brown for his complexion and barely covered the grizzled ends around the base of his head.

"She had craved him all along,"
he said, removing an ice tray from the refrigerator,
"With a passion good and strong.
The fact that she loved him
Was plain to all…"
He handed her a saucer of ice,
"He returned before the dawn
With his coat and trouser torn,
You're a better man than I am
Dizzy Dean."
She threw ice into the tumbler, filled it with gin and shook in some bitters. Poor old bloke, she thought, looking out an office tray. She arranged the drink on a paper towel. and tripped with it to the private office. The chief, sipping, sat in flat-headed contemplation of her. When she had locked the filing cabinet, he collected a despatch case and strutted down the hall, passing Jeremy framed in a doorway.

"Ah Jooning, thought you'd left. Aren't you due at the Argentinian chamber of commerce? What's that you've got? Something for me?"

"Only a draft sir. It'll do for the morning."

"Let me see."

"I was about to put it away."

"Ah. Yes. This one's not current. Must be either Three or Four."

"I was on my way to the shredder."

"But if you were going to shred it, why would it do for the morning? And how could you be about to put it away if you intended to shred it? In fact why shred it at all? Is this a spare?"

"What I meant was I'm on my way to put it away."

"But why take it out at this stage?"

"It was already out."

A keen look came into the chief's eyes as Beula followed the speck-free non-street suit into the public area, "Go and tell Rosario we're coming," he called to Jooning over his shoulder, "and ask if Don Fedoro has arrived and if so we'll take the Rolls." Grapnel put out an arm to Beula, "I wish you were coming to the reception."

*

Dr. Foudroya R was handed out of the limousine by Zeno his chauffeur. In a pale-blue chalkstriped suit, florid tie with diamond pin, the bank director wore the suave, slightly erratic look of the top executive. After greetings, the party got settled into the Rolls, guards in front, Grapnel between Don Fedoro and Beula. While the two chiefs conferred on interest rates, she, without thinking, stretched her arms. Don Fedoro broke off their exchange with, "Are you quite comfortable?" She looked at her lap, wary of signs that Grapnel might be put out by the interruption. In fact, the discussion shifted to road surfaces while the chief regained composure. When the two leaders resumed their dialogue, figures of "nine per cent" and "ten percent" popped back and forth, "I'm afraid," said the oligarch at length, "that nine has to be our ceiling. *Ultima palabra.*"

The chauffeur and two policemen sat like dummies. Beula found herself relaxing, content for the moment to last and last. As the Rolls rounded the bend to where Beula's apartment building stood in its urban meadow owned by the Banco Nacional, Don Fedoro, leaning across the Senior Trade Delegate, said, "I'm having a gathering at Hacienda La Galena this coming weekend. If by any chance you may be free, Doña Beula, we would be honored with your company."

She blushed in confusion, "I think I may...may be free then and...and thank you. Thank you for your kind invitation. I should very much like to come." Had she said too much? Well what the hell.

"She can find her own way down. She's got a mini-car," His Excellency put in with aggrieved cordiality.

"Willis, I wouldn't dream of putting her through those complicated directions. The route peters out after Xavapa. No, I'll send a car on Saturday at 10.30 so she'll be in time for our barbecue in the pinetum. The driver's name will be, let me think, yes, Ramiro."

"Thank you so much, Dr. Foudroya."

After the car door had closed, Fedoro said, "I suppose the LatFrat could live with nine and a half." With a big smile the STD shook Don Fedoro's hand.

20

A tail wind swept Beula along the crazy paving to the front door, driving her up the stairs. It was no good trying to keep a tight grip because elation kept rising and rising. She'd left word for Nolita to go home at 5.30 after feeding the cats and leaving lime juice and ice cubes. With both cats grooming, all she had to do was change for ping pong. She rushed up the five stairs, sprang upon the bed, leapt down then jumped up again. How many women at the secretaries' banquet had actually been included in a house party at Don Fedoro's? It demonstrated what she'd long suspected. She was Preferred and not merely over every other woman at Dimitri's. Recalling Jeremy's expression as she climbed into the Rolls she couldn't help laughing.

The invitation bearing the gold crest of the Banco Nacional arrived next day by hand. Standing on a dining chair Nolita had nearly knocked into the clarkia, trying to identify exactly who had come to deliver it. When would the senorita remember to hand over the two hundred pesos for her eyeglasses? The car was a brand new silver saloon and the driver had not worn a uniform. From where she stood it did not look unlike Don Fedoro himself. The way these under-gnomes try to ape their superiors!

"Here we have the other side of the Big Gap." she told the portera as they fingered the lion and the griffin on the crest, "Most people are impressed with the *Honor Vincit* but I see through it. The great Don Fedoro, son of a retired opera singer from Brooklyn, America. Passable face and voice but an overblown figure and so loud. What could his father have been thinking of?"

The hallmarks of the monied was a topic Nolita and Remedios rarely left alone at their coffee afternoons.

"Despite his fancy manners and the Paris haircuts," Nolita continued, "he'll never manage to cross over into old money. He never makes you feel you amount to anything. Not that he doesn't have charm but it's there for you to admire. Nolita spots new money a mile off. So much gold that for one of his birthdays the family engages a bodyguard, Amo Medianoche, some jumped-up weightlifter. Fedoro's clothes are made in England and Madison Avenue but as Mr. Lanchester said, they could easily have come from Djibouti. With three fountains in front of the town mansion, six amplifiers in the house, two in the library, he must think he's arrived! Everybody knows that getting a brand new car every year is the height of vulgarity. What other proof of recently-arrived is there?"

"Recently-arrived he may be," Remedios cried, "but what wouldn't I give to get my hands on a little of that new money. Just throw some my way."

"They think once they get the electronic doors they're in heaven," Nolita restuck the envelope with care and left it on the sideboard, "Have you ever seen Don Fedoro smile?"

"Was I close enough to see his teeth?"

"*Mira*, I worked in the townhouse nineteen years and I never saw his teeth."

"He has interest in her, no?"

"Interest! His bride has to have lands of her own and be a young virgin. In which case I'm one part qualified," she slapped her haunches, shouting with laughter.

"Wasn't he the one who sent the tree?"

"If you'd learned to read you'd know it was from a gringo."

21

"I now have two vicunas, a pair of orphans airlifted after one of those horrible cullings up on the paramo. I call them Zipaquira and Fusagasuga. They'd like to meet you."

Beula and the North American, Herb Bradstein, sat at one end of the U-shaped dinner table. Don Fedoro at the center of the outer curve kept getting called away. The trip down had been jolting in the extreme, the route after Xavapa nothing but mounds and gulleys. The car Don Fedoro had sent had had good upholstery but something wrong with the suspension. The hutch she'd been allocated, not far from the stables, was perfectly adequate with its own shower and mini-porch, but no window, which meant leaving the door open. Reaching the pinetum in time to see the last of lunch being wheeled away, she'd trekked across the lawns in search of afternoon tea.

A heroic-looking Don Fedoro returned for the cheese course, taking the host seat opposite a top-heavy man with deep-set eyes. Beula's presence, serene yet electric, lit up the frayed-looking company. Every detail, curve of heel in gray velvet pumps, hair that sprang out of her forehead, beaded collar, chiffon gown, concealed a prize out of reach.

"Care for my dessert?" Bradstein asked, "I love halvah but don't digest it too well."

Don Fedoro had not spoken to her over the punchbowl at the get-together after the shoot but seemed overoccupied, hurrying in, hurrying out, disappearing, reappearing in a smoke blue jacket. The elders, surrounding his mother, Doña Clara, in cream satin were considering the advisability of a second serving of milk chocolate pie.

"I'd like to pop over and meet Zipaquira and Fusagasuga," she told Bradstein, "Perhaps in the morning?"

"Believe me, Beula, I'd love to have ya over but it's a little far. Doesn't lie too distant as the crow flies but the road's up where they had the mudslide and it could take several hours. But one weekend, after four dry days, you must come. You'll like the temperature, 70 by day, 50 at sunset." He sat aloof from her looking at his hands, "We're making a plant catalogue. One for slowing heartbeat, another to promote sterility. My plan is to sit out a whole succession."

Wondering what a succession was, she said abruptly, "Did you go to the shoot?"

"I made sure I'd miss it."

She inclined her head as the waiter bent down to tell them coffee was served in the music room. The lights were turned up and couples trailed out of the sala. There must have been a reason why Don Fedoro hadn't said good evening. She'd seen him shake the hand of more than one male guest. Perhaps local protocol had ruled out salutations to single women.

With a sober smile, Bradstein turned to her and crooked his arm. Three harpists were playing airs from the *llanos*, a little bouncy for her mood. From her velvet chaise thoughts drifted to rococo ensembles in pre-revolutionary France. As the trio took a bow, a note was handed to her by one invisible, a sensation not unlike the watch snatch, stealthy, caressing. She turned the note over and made out:

"There's a private party in the little study.
Third on the right after the dining room.
Come alone."

Flushed with pleasure, she now found the music heady. She sat through the encores before asking Bradstein to move his chair. The musicians took a final bow to zealous applause. From the arched doorway Don Fedoro shot glances towards the exit, "I assume you do have time for a nightcap?" he whispered.

Half-smiling she swept behind him along carpeted galleries. At the third door beyond the main hall he halted and stood aside for her to enter, locked the door and turned on a tiny bedside lamp. She was in what resembled a railway compartment with a narrow hospital bed and curtained-off hanging space. Don Fedoro seemed to fill the room. Dragging a nursing chair in front of the door he put his arms around her softly, murmuring, "At last I can speak to you."

It was all happening too quickly for her to experience any stimulus. She had to remind herself who she was with, whose hands had begun searching her breasts, her buttocks, burying themselves in the gray and silver panels, moving down her thighs and up, who it was murmuring,"With you, *querida*, I lose my mind." One hand lifting a diaphanous hem the other searching out her dressfastening, "For you I throw away half a point." His mouth pressing hers, staying in gentle, brazen contact. He smelled of something she could not describe. Remember this is the *jefe estupendo*. He who bankrolled the banquet for ninety-eight women. What would they all say if they knew Himself had sought her out? The room began to overheat. There was a ripping sound as the zip gave out and her dress sank to the floor lying like a storm cloud on the bare boards. It might have got torn but she didn't like to say anything. She could not remember what day of the week it was, let alone any date. At the point of no return he crashed down, slamming her collar bone against the iron bedrail. The pain drove all else from her mind. She managed to raise her head but he came back with more force than before cramping her neck against the bedhead. It's too late, she thought, I could have pleaded a headache. She tried reading his wristwatch but it kept jumping about and anyway it was too dark. She clasped her hands across his back to steady herself, praying for release, to be alone in her hutch with the door locked.

*

Dawn was stealing through a gap in the night sky when she came to. It took several moments for her to recollect where she was. The party had long since dispersed. Sounds of the house were reduced to a distant clatter of plates and occasional voices Muffled birdcalls rose in the semi-dark. Chilly air ruffled the curtain rings. Rubbing her aching head and neck she sat on the edge of the cot, staring at the rag carpet, then felt along the cold floorboards for her dancing slippers, half under the bed, lying in the folds of her gown. Sitting on her knees, she gathered up her dress with its broken zip and took a long time putting it on. Head throbbing, she carefully opened the door and crept down the passage close to the wall.

22

The breakfast table was deserted, very few place settings remaining. Beula poured juice over her cereal and into her coffee. Bradstein, on his way out, did an about turn and pulling out the chair opposite, said "Miz Beula, you look washed out. How was it?"

"How was what?"

"The party I didn't get to go to last night."

"Gruelling if you must know."

"Feel like talking about it?"

"I'd rather not," she rewound her hair, "But I do need to talk. Problem is always what to say."

Bradstein broke off a piece of brioche and sat holding it.

"I've been thinking about Beula Kettlehole," she massaged behind her head, "And what I can say is. She's someone who gets complimented on her outfits. By being mouselike, doors open to her. It all ties in with the passing of time."

Bradstein found her a fresh coffee cup.

"I can't think of any one thing she's good for."

"What about her interests?"

She tore off a piece of croissant and with a bitter laugh, thrust it into her mouth then began to choke. At length she whispered, "Talking of mice, I was at the hairdressers when a field mouse came right out into the aisle. Stopped so close I could see its round eyes and round ears. Then all hell broke loose. Two women climbed onto the wash basins." She put down the coffee cup, "Brad, d'you know I once rehabbed a mouse over the winter. Found her lying on the front lawn. I put her in a secondhand birdcage over the winter and hung it in the window. I knew it was a female because she built a superior nest. In the spring I put her back on the lawn. I only hope she…" her voice tailed off.

Bradstein reached for the milk jug, "She..?"

She shook her head, "I've always fought against…"

Bradstein read the stem of the coffee spoon.

Her napkin was underfoot, "It's…what it is is…fear about…coming over…strong."

He put the spoon back, "Strong?"

She looked at her lap.

"Who says?"

"It isn't just Grapnel. It's…life on someone else's terms. My views are irrelevant. Like the mouse's."

Bradstein, bemused, took out a gold pen and minute pad from an inside pocket, made ticks on it, joining the ticks to make a mini-hexagon, and murmured, "What age group is the boss?"

"Not far off retirement." She reached for the sugar bowl, "Is Gringoland any easier?"

He laughed, "Hardly. But where you're heading will tend to outshine what you left behind."

While she cleaned up the rest of the fruit salad, Bradstein stirred reheated coffee round and round, tasted it and adding more sugar, asked, "Do we have the definition of a kettlehole?"

"It's a water-filled depression left behind by the retreating ice cap."

"Are you, a Kettlehole, going to be content to remain a remnant of patriarchy's Ice Age?"

She stared across the breakfast table to a stuffed shrike under a glass dome, "I never heard of patriarchy's ice age."

"Because, Beula, if you let the patriarchal glacier in the form of His Excellency, or anyone else, encourage you to be a compliant cipher, you'll be helping them make negative templates of what they see as women's role." Around the hexagon he drew a rectangle, "What I'm saying is this. Whatever H.E. may think, you shouldn't hold back from coming over strong on any matter you consider substantive," he wrinkled his small eyes in the smile of a ten year old, as he linked the hexagon to the box.

"In your place, Beula, I'd enlist all the support I need on the road to—I was going to say—declamation," he broke into a titter, "What I mean is the road to articulation." He pocketed the gold pen and notepad, "Don't you realize that what you have to offer is unique?"

She shook her head, "I know I look ghastly."

"I'm talking about who you are, not how you look. Give 'em hell, Beula."

23

"Shall I sugar your tea," Charlotte called over to Elna.

"Yes, if you wouldn't mind. Two lumps."

"Where is she? Charlotte asked, waving a palm at Beula's desk.

"Thursday's her shopping afternoon."

"No, I mean *where* is she?"

"How should I know? With the fugitive from Ecuador. Last Thursday I saw her riding around with Jooning. I thought he'd spotted me but he didn't wave. Anyway when he got to the office, he let drop he'd given her a lift to the dressmakers."

"I see the invitations in her tray."

"Must be the final fling before middle age sets in. I mean, how can she appear with waistlength hair and miniskirts at her age!"

"She doesn't lack for male attention. From Hot Flash down to Juan Minuto," Charlotte said, "Even old Hapkin's in the club. He says most women have shoes like violin cases except her."

"I feel lucky to escape Hapkin's attentions."

"What about Don Fedoro?"

"That I'll never understand. My brother and Lord Ingles would have given their eye teeth to get down to Finca La Galena. I mean, Don Fedoro, usually so protocol conscious! And when his office called the typing room a few days ago asking for her the message was Personal."

They sat sipping tea.

"Elna, what do you make of the 'cultural loan' typo? I mean really. Could it have been she?

"Well it wasn't me, darling! Was it thee?"

*

"If she can't read her notes she should ask. What sense am I supposed to make of this?" The STD looked round at Phuff standing behind, "'The signals in question are to be installed in accordance with the regional balance.' Can you make head or tail of this?"

"Sir, I rushed it in at your request but it isn't really ready for your eyes. It was dictated by Jooning. So let me…"

"But I see it's typed in final form so it is ready for my eyes." Grapnel's stomach lay overfull, dormant. With a sigh he rattled the bottom drawer and pulled out the humidor, "How's that wife of his?"

"Like many of the wives she finds life trying at these altitudes. Still she has her father's visit to look forward to."

"How many directorships has he got?"

"On the board of two banks I'm told."

"Did you hear that she's carrying on with some waiter down in the south end of town?"

"A bit of fleshing out by the myrmidon telegraph. But it might add to the things that worry Jooning."

"Such as?"

"Well, sir, the murder of the Swedish number three."

"Ye-es. Just have a word with Jooning. Grill him on reading his drafts over and over. He shouldn't be allowed to continue on his shaky way. And Phuff, give that typist a second warning from me."

*

Phuff breathed a deep sigh as he closed the chief's door and crossed Charlotte's office to the corridor, heart thawing towards Jeremy. The poor fellow had what amounted to a murky intellect. The so-called brilliance only came in a spark here and a spark there. Jeremy's cubicle was empty, desk disorderly as ever, stack of files on the chair. I ought to have a word with him, Phuff thought, in the nature of a shoring-up. He fingered Jeremy's calendar. In the Gents perhaps. He held the door of his own office, "Ah, just what I'm dying for." He took the teacup and called out, "Charlotte, any sign of the number three?"

"He isn't in," replied Charlotte in a cloud of some late-night essence.

"Where did he get to?"

Charlotte paused, the vapor swirling around them, "Said something about Customs."

"Customs." Finishing his tea, Phuff made his way down the corridor to leave the cup in the guards' lobby, unsettling Luisito at his gluing. Transferring attention to Beula, he strolled across to the typist room with the 'regional balance' letter. The last thing he wanted was to goad her but he ought to put a flea in her ear. Her work standards weren't too far below average, he felt because she was painstaking. How was he going to open the subject? There was the showing at his house of the film, 'Lawrence of Arabia.' Why not begin by inviting her to that? He entered the typist room and looked about. "Where was she?" he enquired of Elna clicking away in her corner. Learning that it was Beula's shopping afternoon, he stood over the diminutive desk and threadbare chair, fingering her velour jacket.

The disclosure engulfed him. He looked up as if in guilt.

24

In order to calm down, Camber decided to work after six. "Don't worry, I'll lock up," he shouted down the corridor to Elna. With the hum of voices diminished, the last staff member out and the lift silent, he was able to make a therapy out of tackling his In Tray. Emotion so pressed in on him that he felt unimaginably feeble, as if his one-engine aircraft had come down in the Baltic and he'd been winched to safety after three hours at sea. The world at large could not be contemplated. He turned off the telephone and sat writing notes to Juan Minuto, initialling drafts for typing. He heard the night porter's whistling but no footsteps so that when Hapkin put a head round the door, Phuff jumped, "Nice evening," he said, in confusion.

"Yus, it'll probably clear up and rain hard."

Dealing with the In Tray Phuff began to feel ever so slightly recovered. After all, Hapkin considers he's a lucky son-of-a-gun to land a life appointment after the death of his wife. And me with Fleur in the summer of her days. Phuff took a few deep breaths, careful not to upset equilibrium, putting newspapers in date order. But thoughts would not be kept out. Opening his desk drawer he removed everything, sharpened every pencil. When Beula's face intruded he penned a note to his mother, commiserating with her colon disorder and recommending a pill used at high altitude. Writing the estate agent about deductions from rent unsupported by invoices, the image of Jeremy and Beula penetrated the rent statement.

"She doesn't want me because I'm married," he said out loud, "She wants him and he's married. *And accompanied.*" He clasped his hands in prayer. We have little in common. She's only good for things fashionable, glamorous. Got herself parked in adolescence, believing all the lotions are made with her in mind. Didn't Jooning say he saw her as overdone? What can he see in her? He addressed the envelope and licked it. If I were a musician I'd sing the Kettlehole Blues. Yes'm, Kettlehole Blues, from mah head to mah shoes…A vision stole up on him. An item on a mantelpiece, half obscured by a marble clock. He got up and charged down the corridor to the STD's office and, closing the door silently, took up the Blue Book. Turning to Support Staff, he began flicking the pages, looking down the K's for Kettlehole.

25

"You're special," Jeremy told Beula as they sped over the top road, beside hedges of bayberry and mountain lilac which kept breaking into narrow vistas of the city hundreds of feet below, past open fields with a shack here and there and at last a view of the great plain. Whiffs of balsawood blew in through the car window.

"I have a feeling you know things," Jeremy announced, "You're not over-educated and the thing that comes through is you Know."

Beula sat in sphinxlike silence.

"You Know," he went on, taking a slow curve without reducing speed, inclining his head towards her, "That the activities we're involved in this fractured time zone, all the luffly luffly partiz, are futile."

She fiddled with her hem. There was an aura of cherry brandy in the car.

"So what level of education did you reach, if you'll forgive my curiosity?"

She put a hand to the neck of her dress, praying that her stutter would sink down, "I...well...I wasn't b-bad at English and French. And latterly Sp-Spanish."

He slowed to fifty at the intersection. "Here one gets bogged down in the two worlds. Work where the office shenanigans help the few keep the masses out of the cash crops. And Home where technically all should be R & R—but isn't for reasons I can't go into. Home more addled than Work even with the locals wheeling in the tea trolley at five and the gin and tonic at seven," he took his eyes from the road, "Am I making sense? It's in taking that step down into the R & R area that one get minced. Trying to hack the concrete, the down-to-earth! There's a lot to keeping feet above ground because it's the coming down that really..." He slowed for the red light and, peering round, went straight into second gear.

Beula laughed, "I never experienced one or the other. Like the ten thousand men."

Putting a heel on the brake, Jeremy turned the squealing car into what looked like a footpath winding through ancient trees. "Your father may drop his aitches. You grew up in a house without a hall. Open the front door and you're in the living room. Yet," the car rocked to a half, "You're illimitable."

They waited as a table was found in one of the bar's dim alcoves. If, in the shimmering deeps, the place looked half empty, the number of waiters in slow-moving silhouette, hinted at innumerable clients in the shadows. Jeremy, eyes in shade, leant on his elbows, "You're surrounded by sidesmen. I tried counting them. There's the youngster, there's the rich gringo. And now the bank boss."

The waiter put down drinks and a dish of pistachios.

"There are other people in the high Andes..."

She sipped from the cuba libre.

"...besides the very young, the very rich and the very powerful."

"The other people are unavailable and I don't see how they can count."

"They don't ask for much. Just to be an invisible hand, a peculiar accessory. Every night at 9 to 9:15 their lambency will be out wavering," he took a gulp from the thick glass, "I know things about you. You don't need a bed to sleep in. You'd doss down on the front lawn and never mind the slugs. Another thing. You don't fit in anywhere. You don't look right. In the office. At parties. Even in the street."

Beula frowned, "Am I any less right than anyone else?"

"Maybe then you're all right everywhere and we others are only all right somewhere."

Beula smiled, showing her long teeth, "It's funny, Jeremy, but because you're out of bounds you're comfortable to be with. At last I feel I can relax."

"Yes relax by all means. Fart, burp and pick your teeth. Look on me as an infirm relative. A large green insect that lives behind your lavatory wall and eats the water blisters."

"The other people hardly need my ministrations."

"Oh Beuly, they would fain."

She sat cooling hands on her glass, "Depending on what's meant by fain."

"They want to be special in their own way. That muchacho squeezing your hand at the Chilean wine-tasting, he probably wants to be special in the usual way. He's handsome."

"I suppose he is in a way, Beula sighed."

"Are you meeting him tonight?"

"For a game of pingpong."

He examined his fingers then drank most of the aguardiente. "You'd rather have him than a teazed out old daddy like me."

Tittering, she signalled to the waiter, "Otra cuba libre por favor."

"What can his rank be?"

"Sounds impertinent."

"Yes Beuly, can you forgive? I want to avoid getting knee-deep in dissonance."

Her profile looked Greek against the bar's undersea lighting, the outline of her pale gold hair shone in new perfection. Her eyelashes, long and darkened, lightly quivered.

"The concern is, how could I have a place in your life?"

"I don't see how, Jeremy." She meant to sound definite, to prevent her lips twisting into unwanted shapes, to stem the caressive impulses coming through like garbled text over the telex.

"...if you could think of me sometimes," he was murmuring, "A few minutes each day, say, between 9 and 9:15 PM?"

The waiter put down more drinks and a dish of pistachios.

"I might," she replied with a sigh, "if not otherwise engaged."

"Engaged?" he said in mock sorrow, "Engaged every minute of every evening? She looked down at her mesh-clad knees for a moment then drew a new wristwatch from some mysterious place, bringing it up close, "But it can't be five and twenty to eight! Have you got the time?"

"Why worry if you're a few minutes late?"

"If I make an appointment I keep it. I must get back before Pablito arrives."

"Is that the chino's name? Who exactly is he?"

Beula started shaking in silent laughter. She put up a hand, unknotted her hair, shaking it to and fro, "Nolita says he's..." she took out a handkerchief, "He's a student of *burrologia*."

"Of what?" Jeremy lifted his glass at the hovering waiter, "What was I having?" he sniffed the glass, "It's full. All right, maestro, no more for the roadbed. Just the *cuenta*. So Beuly, will you keep a special time slot for the other people. Ever?"

26

*J*eremy reached the Import License Commission at ten minutes to ten by the floral clock. Bowing to the sergeant-at-arms who sat cross-legged in a basket chair, Jeremy made his way to the half-door of the anteroom.

"Your pen, wallet and wristwatch if you would be so good," said the constable. He looked new.

"No wallet or wristwatch but," Jeremy held the ballpoint perpendicular. "It's a transistorized pocket mine."

The constable took the pen and returned a battered gambling chip, the ticket to the frisking closet. Usually Jeremy found the ritual faintly amusing, even made an addition to Fleas, Fumes and Flatulence. Today, however, fumbling with buttons and hugging himself in his underwear, he sulked as his suit was engorged into a large mangle. Luckily he'd had the foresight to wear the tan gabardine, in line with the May meeting of commissioners in shades of cafe au lait. Brushing himself down, Jeremy pushed through the fretted doors. The commission were standing about, shifting weight from one leg to the other, all in black.

"It looks as if I might be late," he began, as Don Octavio advanced for the *abrazo*. "Late?" exclaimed the chair in polite bewilderment, "You're not late. But now that you're here we might as well begin."

Don Octavio hurried to the head of the table and with a silver champagne stirrer, tapped on the water glass. Balancing a pair of lunettes he read out the names of those present. Jeremy, half listening, learned that Don Renardo(Customs) was absent and a heavy-set individual was sitting in for him. The chair, a balding young-old man, in a tremulous voice invited all present to his birthday fiesta on the 22nd of July. Jeremy, watching the nose flicker, reminding him of a mini-bosc pear inverted, jumped when he heard the word 'cultural.' It was a word he hoped never to hear again. Was he at the wrong meeting? The back of his neck began to overheat.

The squat new man with quilt button eyes was introduced as head of cultural affairs and Jeremy, putting on a fake smile, recalled the telephone voice which now seemed to be insisting on fees in return for merchandise protection.

"Isn't this Customs' area of competence?" Jeremy put in.

"Customs is a sub-department," replied Amo Medianoche.

Don Octavio went over a list of outgoings connected to the Import License. Police permits, aviation tax, import tariffs, his voice squeaked on, "Totalling fifteen million pesos. Excuse me, gentlemen, I have lost a decimal point. One hundred and fifty million pesos."

The commissioners sat, some doodling. "At the May meeting, I believe the total was under eighty," Jeremy ventured.

Don Octavio returned the look of one who knows all and cannot tell. As they shuffled out, Don Amo brushed up against Jeremy and took his arm, "You may not have heard that Don Renardo seems to be…missing. The LatFrat have designated it as nothing more than dalliance."

"A love affair?"

Don Amo put a heavy arm on his shoulder, "Perhaps, but a love affair with what we are not sure." Nodding over his shoulder, as they strode through the anteroom, his smile widened, "Talking of love affairs, didn't I see you going into the Bar Azulejo with some beauty? Was she by any chance the same blonde I noticed down at Finca La Galena?"

27

*A*fter stewing over the contents of the Blue Book Camber decided to attempt the role of advocate. He had seen the chief off to the heliport to meet Sebastian Xaverel, head of the Metaris Bank and it being the Poison Dwarf's shopping afternoon, followed the tea tray into the typing room. Lounging on a Public Works armchair next to Beula's desk he put one boot on the window sill, referring in an offhand tone to no lack of admirers.

Beula paused in cleaning Grapnel's portable typewriter with an old toothbrush and straightened out paper clip.

"Any more on Bradstein?" Phuff shifted a foot along the window sill nearer to Beula's chair, "Hardly your average American. Careful not to fill in the whole picture," He struggled up and peered out at cloud on the mountaintop, "Would he be some kind of scientist?"

Beula, frowning, said she wasn't sure. Her vowels occasionally let her down, Phuff thought, scraping a spot on his boot. She took uneasy comfort in his presence, baggy suit, pinko complexion, rabbit teeth, straggly hair spread over his crown, even his smell, a mix of earwax and old rail seats; his Englishness, like a tea-cosy bought at Fortnum &

Mason's in the fifties and never dry-cleaned. She was not convinced, though, of his amen to her inaccessibility. In confirmation, his hand reached over and covered hers. Willing Jooning not to look in, with her other hand she went on extracting blacking from 'a' and 'e.' Removing his hand, he sat back in the gray vinyl chair.

"I don't want to sound like a dutch uncle," he said, giving a flick to the cat mobile overhead, "But do you have a father?"

"Died last year."

"What work did he do?"

"In the provisions business."

"Groceries and comestibles?"

"Smoked meat."

"Siblings?"

"A brother I never see."

"Any close relatives?"

"I've never been one for family."

"Any late family?"

"My grandmother was an ally. Died two years before my father "

He perched on the window sill, "Don't let's be trapped into believing that after today it's all plain sailing." His smile was tentative, "You're a lovely lady. Now. But you don't need me to remind you what are a girl's best friend."

Furiously Beula scrubbed the blackened toothbrush on an ancient blotter.

"Who'd be up to doing another tour at this altitude? Aside from earthquakes and open drains, haven't you worried about being in the path of a stray bullet? I have many a time," he retied his boot, "Ask yourself what you'd be giving up. I mean to say what else is here for you? Married men stay married."

Beula stopped wiping her fingers on the blotter then leaned forward, "You're not hinting by any chance? At something between me and a married man?"

"Did I say that?"

"Why even mention it?"

A fly flopped on the window pane. Phuff opened the casement to let it out. "It doesn't matter to me what you get up to on your shopping afternoons. I just hope the boss doesn't get wind of it."

She looked ahead, long and hard, then broke out, "Why hasn't it ever occurred to anybody that there might be more to Beula Kettlehole than...than m-m-mere physical comfort?"

"My dear, you're not making the slightest sense. I believe in you. That's why I'm urging you to consider this Bradstein chap."

"I'm tired of seeing any prospect with money as a prize. Isn't it about time someone thought of *me* as a prize?"

"Plant your feet on the ground, Beula. It's no good getting a swollen head over Don Fedoro." As he eyed her over the teacup she felt a twinge. Has he looked me up?

That leaves you with the manikin. Pablito is it? He's the type that...Could I also have a cup, not so much milk this time?...the type women go for in their dotage." He transferred from Elna's chair to the window ledge, "Getting back to Brad, what do we know of the cove?"

As Camber waited, they heard Hapkin droning in the public office.

She rummaged in a small red tin box of paper clips for a pin, "Bradstein spoke out against patriarchy. Says it's a glacier and I'm not to let it put my personal development on ice."

"Still," he added more tea to his cup, "If you play your cards right you might find yourself living on Fifth Avenue, Manhattan. If I were you I'd go to work on him. Bearing one's shelf life in mind." Laying the rattling cup and saucer on the trolley, he wrinkled his nearly black eyes, "Now I wonder if I could give you this letter. You'll never be able to read my scribble. To Jorge Ramirez. Jay Oh Are Gee Ee. Are Eh Em Ay Are Ee Zed. Copy title and address from this letter. Dear Dr. Ramirez, we return herewith your plans for work on the west window of..."

*

The rain sweeping across the Carrera had had the usual effect of halving traffic volume. Windscreen wipers were routinely snapped off by the practised hands of gamines pretending to clean windshields. A pair huddled in a cardboard box down by the traffic light. A third shinned up the lamppost. Seven floors above, Beula stood glued to the window, watching for Jeremy's car to draw up on the other side of the Carrera, a sign that she had five minutes to lock up, run down seven flights and cross the street. Except for the TV aerial flashing red in the mist, rain had blotted out the mountain. She and Alf Hapkin were quite alone. Locking herself in the typing room, she climbed into her beaded cocktail dress.

Ten minutes later still no car. Up to now she'd taken for granted that Jeremy would always show up. But Camber's lecture had left her unable to bounce back into unthinking calm. Imagining the Lagonda might never slide into its space, anguish rose from nowhere. The Carrera turned into a river, the Magdalena, usually lying like a great dun-colored snake nine thousand feet below the altiplano, and Beula wading beyond pleasure craft, sinking into the deeps where memories sail by like filmstrips.

Six thirty. Sighing, she turned her back on the to-ing and fro-ing of twin orange headlights and walked towards the spotted mirror behind the steel press. The vision had a lopsided look, one eye glad, the other troubled. She pressed the lock on the gray filing cabinet. Was it only last night that Grapnel drove her off in the red Mercedes leaving the detectives standing? You should have seen their faces, she told the wall calendar.

The night watchman vocalized in the public office:

"I'll be seizing you…"

"Good night Mr. Hapkin," she called out.

His head popped up, puffy round the eyes, "You can call me Alf. There's no extra charge." She watched him stir cocoa into a tiny milk saucepan, his toupee barely covering grizzled sideburns. Holding a fork parallel to his eyes and sliding his jaw back and forth, he said, "Tell me, are the natives friendly?" She stood back as he unbolted the front door. "Abyssinia," he added as she left.

*

In the rain and the dark, pedestrians gathered in the main doorway. Edging her way through a crowd smelling of old overcoats, she stood on tiptoe to peer across the Carrera. No car. Twirling her waxy umbrella, she was soon accosted by a small child with a man's face peeping out from under a homburg. His eyes reflected the street lights as he grabbed the note she saved for beggars and hobbled away, his black trench coat dragging in the wet. She wasn't going to hear Jeremy's plea that the field of geopolitics wreaked havoc on his private life.

Between the heads under the pastry shop awning she heard the high-pitched burble of an elder, "*Me regala alguna cosita, me hace el favor.*" Again she fished under her ruana and brought out another five peso note. Someone was chuckling and she looked up to see Jeremy's hand outstretched, "*Se me regale a mi, a mi.*" He had a way of cancelling his vibrations. Under the umbrella wedged against the wall he took both her hands, "It's my predilection for excitement. And excitement is you. You." He waltzed them out to the curb, "Sometimes," he whispered into the driving rain, "When I want to be by myself, I go to a secret place and relive our moments together. If I didn't put in some discipline I'd be thinking of you all day."

"What about thinking of keeping an appointment," she said in a mock moue, "The illimitable one has not got illimitable time."

"Well," he nuzzled her hand, "I had to drop off the mad parson and the food. The gamines were at the ready. By then I'd lost my parking spot. Beula, I know you can forgive the delay because you're made for Greatness. Most women, Rowena included, believe in the palpable. You go to work, you earn money, you pay bills. The Muse sees beyond. I don't suppose she ever reads anything," he shouted as they tore across the Carrera against the lights. "And why should she?" he breathed as they reached the car park, "The Muse doesn't need facts cluttering up its plans because it Knows." He shook her by the shoulders, "I'm humbled by the quality of our happiness." He peered between the parked cars to check that Jorge the chauffeur had left for the day, "I fantasize about your petticoats and congratulate myself that there by the grace of God go I."

In the fast lane they travelled the autopista, straddling some potholes, impacting others, "I've something of consequence for us. Listen carefully. Rowena's been seen entering some waiter's apartment, Antonio Rueda by name. Going in at three, coming out after five. It looks as though we might get her on that."

"But Jeremy when it comes down to it, would divorce really be…be on the cards?"

"Not to worry, you won't be cited. Oh my dearest one, why are you trembling?"

"Us?" Beula sank back into the upholstery with Jeremy clasping her hand, his pale eyes calm with sweet happiness. Traffic had suddenly become heavy. The car slowed down and after moving five yards in as many minutes, stalled in a long line. From an adjacent car they learned of a roadblock half a kilometre ahead.

"Another accident?" Beula wondered.

"No darling. They're searching cars. A body, found three days ago on Calle 72, had a car license number in a pocket. Not a foreigner, thank God."

The line started moving. Jeremy put the Lagonda in motion, turned off the highway onto parkland and bumped up the hill. Soon they were speeding along the top road winding between squatters' huts on the upper slopes and high-rise apartments below. The roadside, faintly lit from the plain below, made all appear romantic. Opulence and eyesore lay cloaked under lanterns and floodlit bushes. The moon raced behind trees whose elongated shadows swivelled across a silver screen and spun round in a fan across the windshield. Beula relaxed under the

sedative effect of the purring engine, giving herself up to the enchant-
ment of the moment.

At the corner of Calle 60, Jeremy clasped her hand, "Remember,
whatever happens, we're one. I'll be over for a word before supper. Look
for me under Bolivar's statue—the long lean one, facing the main staircase. At nine."

Beula tap-tapped along the edge of Don Octavio's urban estate amid
vistas of floodlit, miniature hills and valleys beyond the wire fence. She
was certain she'd heard right for he had said it. HE had said THEY had a
chance. How do I know I'm not dreaming? She crossed the wet verge to
hug a steel fencepost and marvel at its sliminess, to stroke a hornbeam
leaf, shiny and saturated. Rowena may all the time have been hoping for
some excuse to bow out. How to face Rowena though? Once or twice
she'd had to struggle with insecurity when Jeremy caught his wife's eye.

Beula flounced past security guard and watchdog. A liveried maid
took umbrella and raincoat, carefully lifted off her poncho and helped
with pendant, earrings and bangle, directed her to follow a stick of a girl
with dotted complexion through a colonnade to the main hall, teeming
with the young, the young-looking and the beautiful, a near mono-
chrome display of black and cream, men in silks and linens, women in
faille and chenille.

"Ah Beula." The number one, noting her smile, encircled her, "What a
dazzling dress."

"I say," Phuff murmured through the roar of voices, "If you're not
doing anything later we might go on somewhere."

Bemused she made her way to the edge of the crowd, spotting Jeremy
talking to a tall, bald man and Rowena with a notice on her chest.

The doctor says my throat will be finished Saturday.

Until then I'm speechless. So please take care of me and give me a drink.
Mrs. J.

"Rowena," Beula said in her ear, "I'm sorry about your throat. You
look marvellous in shades of cream."

She whispered, "Jeremy says he's enjoying the hushed mode." With a penetrating look she joined the circle around Grapnel.

In a far corner Don Fedoro bent over a young woman whose dark hair fell below her hemline. Glancing behind, he caught sight of Beula, and made his way over with his blend of excessive courtesy and intemperate determination.

The lights dimmed. A spotlight went on and off before hovering on the host, Don Octavio, gold tonsured, pince-nezed, waving for silence. There was laughter at his announcement that the band would play only till suppertime because unlike making love, dancing is best enjoyed on an empty stomach. Musicians in purple satin, after a few peeps and rattles, struck up the hit tune, 'My Brother's Wake,' whose melody and beat sent electric currents through the party. Guests swarmed onto the dance space, drawn into a rhythmic whirlpool wiggling to beat of shaker and scraper.

Fedoro emerged beside Beula and took her arm. Dancers made a path for them to the center of the floor. Fedoro looked strained, his eyes fixed Beula with peculiar intensity, "You dance well," he said, drawing her near and she, aware of rivalry, whispered, "It may look easy, but you'd be surprised how many hours it takes getting it right."

He looked rueful, then smiled and began chuckling. He had a sense of the beat yet his way of bounding back and forth on one foot made her hip ache. She broke away to dance solo, the better to show her style. At the edge of the floor, Jeremy stood with the Metaris Bank's number three. Suddenly, he threw his glass at the wine waiter and plunged onto the floor, seizing Beula by the wrists.

"You're driving me mad," his look always guarded, betrayed emotion.

She danced a few steps then gently unclasping herself, pushed him away and turned to Fedoro, who held her too tight, making her dress wrinkle and ride up, "I wonder if you know, Miss Beula," he murmured, "that to desert a partner in the middle of a dance is not usual."

"He's from the office."

"What has that got to do with it?"

"He might-might have thought it was an old fashioned excuse-me dance."

"He didn't cut in on his grandmother. Clearly where protocol is concerned he's a boor. But you moved with him. And I saw the looks he gave you."

"I get an admiring look now and then."

"It went a few steps beyond. It told me certain things. Things that only you knew."

Beula began to giggle with a shaky jaw, "Mr. Jooning's wife is here tonight. Over there, the lady with the notice." She wanted to excuse herself but knew she should not. Trying to sound firm yet breezy, her voice came out an octave higher, "I don't know what you think you're imagining, Don Fedoro."

"I'm not imagining anything."

She threw her head back and he saw how exactly the reality of her met his fantasy. Her Grecian profile, eyes set on the slant, the fluidity of her thick gold hair, could cause him to lose his mind. Had he been too insistent down at the finca? He'd drunk too much. But, having dared to attract him so blatantly, what did she expect, a few kisses on the pergola? If it was good five weeks ago tonight will be even better. She has all the endowment, all the helplessness for la ultima experiencia.

"You never returned our phone call?"

"What phone call?"

His eyes softened, "I can't take you home this evening," he said, not letting go of her wrist, "But I will visit later on tonight."

Too uneasy to meet his eye, yet at some deeper level in her element, she took a breath, "I don't think…Well, what I mean is, the front door gets bolted at midnight and…and the p-portera has to get up at…at-at five." She excused herself and tried to get past. The pain jolted her into memories of her grandmother's words. Words she had not then understood about mishandling the face of passion. Acquittal called for inferior postures. Arriving at a tryst in stained clothing accompanied by a beauteous friend, talking with one's mouth full. "I'll never see twenty-one again," Beula announced, "I haven't a p-penny to my name. Just the c-c-clothes on my back." She looked down willing him to relax his grip until she felt something warm from behind and Jeremy, a little out of breath broke in between them.

"Evening Fedoro. I'm just about to send Rowena home. Her sore throat'll never mend in all this smoke. That, plus a bout of altituditis seems just about to have caved her in. I'll probably cut short my dinner with Delacourt and try to have an early night."

Fedoro smiled in his elliptical way, making Jeremy relax, "Talking of having an early night, I was just asking our friend Beula here, how it is that when it comes to sharing her out, my share should be so skimpy?"

Jeremy's eyes flashed danger. Then he grinned, "Beula's our amanuensis so to request a share of her services, I suggest you address yourself to the Assistant Trade Delegate."

"I saw you on the dance floor."

Jeremy stepped back to let Beula pass and a bevy of dinner guests through.

"I saw you," Fedoro repeated over the din.

"Yes, Don Fedoro, I saw you."

"Don't be funny with me, Mr. Jooning."

"I'm not being funny but let me say this. At some parties there's a custom of asking every lady in turn to dance."

"I've seen you at all kinds of parties and I never once saw you dance with any lady, not even your wife."

"I think I'm entitled to ask whose business it is if I dance with my wife or not."

"What we're talking about is dancing with other...ladies," he leant against Jooning, "I've never seen you dancing with any lady at all."

"Are you sure you're feeling all right?"

"You were just a little while ago dancing with Her."

"You're telling me I've got no right to dance with an office typist?"

"There are two factors here. One, from my observation of you, you don't as a rule dance at all. Your lack of skill at the cumbia is only too obvious. Two, your absence on the floor at my mother's birthday fiesta, even for the last waltz, made me…"

"Fedoro please, I meant no insult to Doña Clara."

"…made me wonder. Either he's uncomfortable with the waltz or didn't want to bother to grant the occasion respect." Fedoro grabbed Jeremy's arm above the elbow, "I'd like to believe the former, that you don't dance at all. So on that score I could forgive you. But that you should cross the floor and deliberately cut in on me is a breach of…"

"Oh is that all!" Jeremy had started to tremble all over."

"You raise your hand like this," Fedoro stepped back and lifted one hand in a Statue of Liberty pose, "And she's all eyes for you. I see sparks flying out of the overheated furnace. I see all and I know all. Driving down the mountain in separate cars, one arriving at the hotel at eleven in the morning, the other at two in the afternoon. Both missing from the bathing party next morning. La Beula showing up for lunch an hour early to put the others off the scent." Jeremy took a step back, "Your awkwardness about an introduction never rang true."

"Don Fedoro, please. I am not Pelleas. Neither am I Tristan. Between myself and Ms. Kettlehole there is no overheating boiler. I wish I had time for a few dreams around the couches of the Hotel Guadaira, let alone live them. She's an attractive enough woman if you say so but be assured that I have not the least inclination towards La Beula, as you call her. So rest easy and if I…"

"You've been seen together drinking at Jokers Point."

"Pure fiction."

"Well Mr. Jooning, be aware that if we discover the two of you, we shall be over to make ourselves known."

*

Two footmen pulled open white and gold doors and the supper room lay unattended. Banks of soft mauve flowers, silver pedestal dishes piled with red and green delicacies, white and gray china bowls and plates, crystal goblets and decanters glinted under the candelabra. A couple lingered in the doorway. In no time diners were blocking the entrance. Over the tops of bobbing heads, slivers of meat, pink, beige and red, seemed to reach halfway to the chandelier. It became impossible to move without being squeezed by bodies as fragrant as flowers, a parade of beaded purses, silk shirts and bobbing pendants.

Beula edged her way carefully through the crowd. A path opened for the lodestar caressed by the arms and eyes of new acquaintances. Don Octavio took her elbow and piloted her to the supper room. General Tazul's pale eyes darkened as she brushed his girth. At her hemline there was rustling. Looking down she found Jeremy, on his knees, hardly reaching to her armpit. Not responding to laughter he whispered, " Face the table and listen. Meet me at the third pillar from the statue."

"When?"

"Now," He slid a fork from the table and slipped into the crowd.

"I believe that's peppermint aspic," Phuff said, handing her a plate, "How about a spot of that with Pasta Barbarella?"

Muttering 'powder room,' Beula ducked behind a large woman in a cloak trimmed with what looked like human hair, and made her way to the colonnade, hesitating at the third pillar and Jeremy's beckoning.

"Now Beuly, can you concentrate? Fedoro has been sounding off. Have you…did you ever…encourage him?"

"I don't consider I did."

"He's in a strange mood. Stand in the shadow more. You may know he's the main player in this transaction."

"Which transaction?"

"The one with all the drafts," he looked behind him, "I wondered if you wouldn't mind going home early?"

"How early?"

"Now."

"Well I would mind. Why would you even suggest that?"

"Because it's business."

"Why didn't you think of business when you cut in on the dance? No, Jeremy, you can't push the Muse around like this," she moved into the light and he pulled her back.

"The deal affects us both now. We'll speak at eleven," he cupped her face, "Under this pillar."

*

"We must bear in mind," Grapnel told Pike Xaverel, head of the Metaris Bank, "That at Finca Galena only last week, there was a third incident in three weeks. One of Fedoro's oldest retainers shot at close range. Returning with the wages."

They hovered on the threshhold of the supper room, bowing as fragments of the glittering company slipped by, two elders, one middle-sized and overweight, the other diminutive, in nearly identical suits. At a bow-fronted window displaying floodlit roses and gardenias, they settled on a table. A waiter scampered over.

Lighting a cigar, Grapnel congratulated the banker on speed of arrival and smooth flight.

"Insofar as we didn't scrape any of those cockscomb peaks," Xaverel smiled briefly, "Willy we're not displeased with the nine and a half," he stirred the espresso, "But that doesn't mean we're going to lend one penny against outrageous protection payouts. All I'm hearing is another forty million here, fifty million more there and now this monstrous demand for seventy million. I tell you, the antics of this Midnight thug could well put the kibosh on any more dealings with the LatFrat."

"Pike, you have my word that we're doing all we can to get Medianoche removed from the import license commission, not physically of course, hahaha."

"And what about tonight's how d'ye do? I had to be brought in by 'copter. Come on Willy, let's have it."

"Body parts around a parked car. Customs officer. Dead three days at least. Yes I will have a spot more more coffee. Tiny drop of milk, not cream."

"I heard it had to do with Mr. Midnight."

"Really!" the STD feigned a yawn, "Well, Don Renardo did insist all protection fees were to go to them." He winced as the trouser dress seam cut into his groin, "I doubt Medianoche's involvement somehow. Nevertheless one can't neglect precautions. I now use a different car every day, take varying routes home. Stick with the guards."

Pike Xaverel poured out more espresso, "What with the Uzi and the burp gun you should be covered. And you've got the blonde vanguard."

"You heard about that?" Grapnel stretched over to the decanter, "It seemed the sensible thing. They see a woman in the car and think twice. On the curbside for visibility, next to Julio. He's careful to keep the weapons bag away from her feet." He drank down the rest of the port.

"You mustn't worry so much, Willy."

In the roar of voices the chief signalled to Jooning, "What's all the brouhaha?"

"The toast, sir." A cluster of waiters, poised on either side of the doors, balanced trays of champagne.

"You'd think," Grapnel groaned, "they'd invent some sort of new drink. One gets awfully bored with pink champagne, d'you find?" Their voices were drowned in the chanting, "Felicitades, felicitades." Reluctantly they got to their feet and followed the diners to the dance space to join circles around Don Octavio, the clockwise inner ring, anti-clockwise outer ring, the clockwise outer outer ring.

*

Beula, caught in a dialogue between Don Amo of Cultural Affairs and Don Felipe of Aviation, unclasped the latter's fingers and backed out of the group. At the edge of the dance floor a pair of chestnut eyes swept the company. The rest of the face was blocked off by Grapnel's wife's hairpiece. Mumtaz Grapnel moved, revealing the familiar shaggy haircut and three-piece suit. The chestnut eyes found hers, narrowed and Pablito stepped into view to lead Beula to the floor. At the end of the set, Pablito bowed. Beula left him and walked towards the table where sat Xaverel, Don Fedoro, Grapnel and numbers two and three. All five diners rose, making a great clatter. With a half-tipsy smile, she waited while a place was made between Phuff and Xaverel. Jerking a head towards Beula, the STD murmured, "Pike, here's your chance to dance with our blonde bombshell."

"Dance?" Xaverel looked incredulous, "All I ask is that I'm returned to my hotel in one piece when you fix up the transport. By then I'll hope to reach some sort of amnesty with my stomach."

"I told Beula," Phuff began in a chatty domestic tone, "That she isn't eating properly. Needs filling out a bit."

"Looks comely enough," the chief, murmured, scanning the horizon, "Ready Pike?" Shoulder to shoulder and deep in dialogue they moved away.

*

As they were lost to sight, a golden hand laid itself on Beula's shoulder. She jumped, then with an automatic smile, said, "Do you all know Don Pablito?"

"How d'ye do?" said Camber without offering a paw. Jeremy nodded into his glass and Fedoro looked up darkly, "What did he do, climb in through the scullery window?"

Pablito all smiles, pulled out a chair and wiggled into Xaverel's place.

"He must have come in with the fish delivery."

Pablito put an elbow on the table, "I come alone."

"Yes," Fedoro resumed, "And someone put in the good word?" He jerked a thumb towards Beula, "Was it her?"

Beula rose, articulating need for a peppermint. In mannequin tread, she glided in the direction of the powder room.

"From the way you're comporting yourself it seems to me that you know her at least as well as the rest of us," Fedoro announced.

Jeremy slowly got up, strolled over to the bar and picked up a syphon of soda. Sliding it onto the table he said in mock cheerful tones, "Well don't we all look tense! Why all the bloody drama?"

Nobody uttered a word, nobody looked up. At length Pablito spoke. "It's Beula he's preoccupied about."

"Yes," Fedoro said in bitterness, "You think she might be your nookie, you stunted little dago, well she isn't, she's everybody's nookie."

Jeremy put a thumb on the soda spritzer and the others froze. Under scrutiny he hesitated. Phuff leant across a corner of the table and put a hand behind Fedoro's lapel, "People are starting to look round. I wish we knew what you're so uptight about?"

Pablito spoke again, "It's her He want to make love with her after hours and he can't."

Fedoro looked round and started to chuckle in bursts and wheezes, "I've changed my mind about this chino. Let him stay. Tell me, court jester, for a woman on the wrong side of forty is she an acceptable lay?"

"Well," Pablito reported, "She does not need a bar of soap."

Fedoro began shaking with laughter, "Oh that, my friend, that's precious. She doesn't need a bar of soap!"

The silence around the table got cumbersome. Phuff's face turned a shade of pink matching Grapnel's own. "Discussing an employee." he muttered, "as one would a...commodity?"

"Senor Phuff, don't tell me what I may say and what I may not say. The woman's a tart."

"She is not a tart."

"The woman's forty-five all got up to look twenty-five," Fedoro declared, thumping on the table, unsettling the champagne glasses.

Phuff held up a hand, "Let's try to avoid...upset."

"I am upset," Fedoro relaxed his hold on the table to summon the waiter and whisper in his ear, then turned to the company "If we can't settle it here, there's elsewhere. And if not now. Later."

"But Fedoro," Jeremy had difficulty getting the words out, "Would you mind telling us why this censure is aimed at a UK-based member of our delegation? Why not at Maribellita or Consuelo?"

Eyes rested on Fedoro frowning into his drink. After several weighty moments, he spoke, "What it comes down to gentlemen, is this. Which one of us is going to escort her home? My turn came some weeks ago," he scanned each face, "Reports reach me of certain activities. She drinks at the Bar Azueljo Mondays evening. Visits Tierra Caliente with one nameless. Entertains at home various classes not excluding the shanty town." He glared up from under his brow, "What I wonder is, am I being passed over on the roster?" He bit a thumbnail, "We get tired of establishments like Doña Sofia's. Every other woman we know has either a husband or a mother." He put out an arm and swept champagne glasses and ashtrays onto the carpet.

What followed resembled well-rehearsed steps in an ancient ritual. Phuff pulled a crumpled handkershief from his trouser pocket and mopped the polished table then, with a flourish, brought another handkerchief out of his top pocket, unfolded it and dousing it with soda water, dabbed at Fedoro's sleeve. Jeremy, checking to see if anybody had marked the incident, signalled a waiter to clear the table. Pablito bent down and picked up every cigarette butt that had slipped down between the chairs, wrapped them in a cloth napkin and put them in his pocket. At the center sat Fedoro, silent, speculative, smoking. Don Amo appeared and stood behind his chair.

*

The powder room was so congested that Beula could not get an uninterrupted view of herself. Partial vistas, however, radiated a yard-high magnetic field, her imago achieved. Sprinkling *Nuits de Tanger* behind ears she took stock of the situation. Jeremy. He'd already made one false move. Better take some soundings. She pulled open the velvet door, letting a flurry of young women in. Guests saying their good-nights caught her up in the drift towards the front hall. After a glance at the grandfather clock pointing to three minutes to eleven, she spotted Jeremy and Phuff at the Salvador statue, Jeremy downcast until his bald-headed financier appeared. Accompanied by Don Amo, Fedoro put a hand on Jeremy's shoulder with a remark that made them all burst into rueful laughter, then marched off leaving Jeremy and Delacourt arms linked walking round in a circle. Camber had faded from view.

How would she get home? She didn't fancy a two-mile hike with Pablito. Camber? All right, one brandy alexander at the Zonatricia. But no dancing. As women in fur stoles climbed into the endless carousel of transports, she got close enough to the open doors to feel a sudden chill. Rummaging in pockets for a scarf, she positioned herself by the third column, keeping a lookout for Jeremy.

Fedoro's limousine was rounding the bend, the shiniest in the line idling under the portico. Slowly it moved up. Don Amo held the rear door open as the bald man and Jeremy hurried through the crowd. Then, Fedoro himself got out, giving an auctioneer's nod, making a shutter movement to one invisible and Phuff, raincoat under arm, rushed out as if catching the last bus. The Rolls glided into gear and as it began circling the driveway, Pablito, appearing from nowhere, ran with it as it gathered speed. The braking light went on and Pablito, still running, jumped up and clung on like a gamine.

28

"In any case, Harry," Jeremy murmured, "Choir cannot be scheduled · for the next week or two. You may or may not be aware that Phyllis is the dynamo as far as the hall rental goes but unfortunately she's booked up at all hours. No she can't give a date for the next rehearsal. But she will call to confirm. Harry are you there? You see it came to Phyllis's attention that the Moorish Saloon is no longer available to us. Why? Well there are better acoustics down in the Gran Comercio…Yes I suppose Phyllis could give one or two choir members a lift home…Look, on second thoughts they'd better bring their own transport. Phyllis says two weeks time. Earlier? Out of the question. Space must be found for the choir."

Beula listening to this farrago, said in an agitated voice, "Is Phyllis all right?"

"After a moment of hesitation, Jeremy resumed in breathy tones, "Look here, Harry, last night Phyllis could hardly meet the organist's eyes. She was asked for an account of her delay and she had to explain about dropping off a new hymn with the parson. The trouble was the organist had already tried to call…"

"The organist?"

"Yes. In trying to reach Phyllis at her office, he learned that Phyllis had already gone to choir and was expected to go onto Customs after half past three. The organist called again after four but no Phyllis. Now," Jeremy said, "this is the crux."

Beula held her head.

"Believe it or not, the organist actually put in a call to Customs asking for Phyllis and was told that our bass Don Renardo had been dead six days. Phyllis was hard put to explain why she was expected that afternoon. To crown everything the organist asked after Harry. So that is in essence why rehearsal has to be postponed. Phyllis's stomach is hanging by a thread

*

Two weeks later Jeremy was on his way to an assignation with Beula at the Salvador Hotel. Wherever possible he avoided driving through city traffic, mainly autos of American make—cabin-sized wrecks dating back to the fifties—and battered, rusting charabancs, proceeding at no more than twenty miles an hour. Not that sluggish chaos in any way lessened the risk of collision. There was nothing to deter a bus driver from denting a car broadside as he changed lanes. One of these behemoths overtaking Jeremy let fly a blast of exhaust that enveloped the Carrera in yellowish gray miasma. Keeping a decent distance between the bus's bumper and the bonnet of the mini, Jeremy reduced speed to twelve.

Damn, why had he offered to collect Rowena's mini? Was he being punished for duality? Would the bus never make its turn? For a few blocks he suffered until, with another tremendous burst of flatulence, the bus accelerated short of the Salvador hotel and swung left into an arclike intersection. Now all he had to do was roll round and round the car park ramps to a place far from prying eyes. A muscular teenager arose out of the gloom, assuring Jeremy of the car's chances of remaining unmolested, and pledging for an extra five pesos to remain on guard for however long the senor might wish.

*

The smells of the grand hotel: chocolate, perfume, new carpeting rose in welcome and reassurance. Passing the emerald boutique, Beula slackened her stride to acknowledge the glances of the armed guard. Having declined to meet in the Gran Comercio, she had, with Jeremy's uneasy acquiescence, selected the hotel's Bar Intima. One or two peeps at the macrame wall-hangings, a few steps round the bend in the corridor and she'd be There where moments of towering grandeur were lying in wait. Terracotta lamps shed tiny beams to enable the clientele to see their drinks. Counting alcoves, Beula stopped at the fourth from the end. Jeremy, without getting up, silently pushed the table out for her to fit into the booth. With his face obscured, she had to guess at his mood. No, his stomach was more or less quiet after the party, and yes, Rowena's sore throat had mended. Had he managed to find out anything more about Antonio was her next feeler. Her eyes had got used to the semi-dark and she saw no recognition of her meaning. He waved to the waiter, and smiled mechanically as he gestured towards her, Cuba libre or B.L.S.?"

"I think I'd like cognac."

"Bueno Hector, one Martell and same again for me. Now, which Antonio are we talking about?"

"Antonio, the lover."

"Oh," he sighed, "*That* Antonio. By the way, while I think of it, if you insist we meet here, can you do something about your hair? Don't think I don't love it, the way it floats about. It just, well, makes us visible. Can't you tie it up or something, out of sight?"

From her bag on the floor she reached down and brought out a black band of chiffon, tying it round her head twice.

"Now you look like Beula La Zingara." Seeing her expression settle, he looked into his drink and reached into a pocket, "Antonio," he turned the name over in his mind as if trying to unearth some ancient formula, "Antonio?" he repeated, bringing out a packet of Turkish cigarettes. "What I'd managed to find out is that he happens to live in the same building as her dressmaker so she might have an alibi." Looking past her he surveyed the bar at large like an actor trained to sway an audience, "In any case," he sighed, "I doubt it's true."

"The fact of her meeting him isn't true?"

"Don't see how it can be, sweetie-heart. She's been looking wretched lately. Seems prickly for no reason. Hardly symptoms of the woman in love. Doesn't have your radiance. Whenever I get back she's home. I rather fear the Antonio business may have been wishful thinking. But we love each other. We'll find a way."

"Are you saying that for us you don't see, well, permanence as a p-possibility?"

"Did I say that?"

Beula's drink remained untouched, "I want to ask you something."

"You don't have to get permission."

"Supposing you'd never met Rowena, what sort of woman would you have wanted to spend your life with?"

"Poppet, I can't answer that."

"If-if-if you'd never met her, would you have considered…Me?" She sat up straight, breathing hard.

"Haven't I already said so? The reality is I'm married to someone brought up a Catholic. Her father…"

Her father, Beula shouted to herself, as the explanation unfolded. Why did he never mention his wife without bringing in her father? Papa's a Catholic. Papa's got bursitis.

"I had a friend once," she said, swallowing half the brandy, "Valkyra Martensis."

"Well well."

"I know your resistance to hearing about people you don't know."

"It's hard enough to work up interest in the ones I know."

"I won't stretch it out."

"Dearest, you never speechify. Okay, what about the war maiden?"

Beula leant forward. With the black scarf tied piratewise and her great eyes looking into the balloon glass, she reminded him of a geomancer on Clacton pier,"Valkyra used to go on and on about her mother. Recognition of accomplishments. 'Mother cut the grass all by herself,' or 'Mother's taken to wearing bicycle clips in the rain.' That's not a very good example."

"What about, 'Mother drove a five-ton lorry through the Pennines on the ice?'"

"That's going too far. I know, 'Mother makes whortleberry pies with her own hands.'"

"Hector," his eyes got round when he smiled. The waiter in an instant was there with "*Que les provoca?*" Ordering same again, Jeremy put out his cigarette, "Darling, I can't stand the suspense."

"Spare me the sarcasm."

"It's not meant to be sarcasm."

"I may not have put it well. There were other instances. She never said, 'Mother's taken up flying,' because that'd be laying it on. Wait," she raised her glass, "'Mother drives in all weathers.' Most people have no choice but Valkyra's mother didn't have to. Over the years it came to me that she was talking not about mother but about money." Beula sipped from the balloon glass, "No one whose parent works as a fairground attendant goes into details of mum's driving skills or mum's pie-making." Beula emptied the glass, "How well off is her father?"

"Whose?"

"Rowena's."

"On the board of one or more banks."

"Would you rather have eloped or met the girl's father first?"

"I suppose the latter."

"If he'd worked on the Big Dipper, would you have married him?"

"The what?"

"The way you seem to be married to the banker."

"Married to the banker! It would be funny except…he mumbled into this glass then fell silent, finally saying, "I think we ought to get going. Did you bring your car?"

"I don't want to ruffle you," her great eyes shone, "But you do things that ruffle me. Ordering me home from Don Octavio's."

Jeremy's sat expressionless.

"Something was said that night."

"Was it?"

"Well wasn't it?"

He moved the small lamp, "I don't feel you pay enough attention to protocol. I mean if you will conduct yourself like an *ingenue libertine,* tongues are going to wag. None of the women seem to like you."

Lines appeared round her mouth, "Something was said at the party, wasn't it?"

"You must know."

"Did my name came up?"

"No," he replied after a pause, "It was all business."

"Do you want us to stay together?"

"I do," He nodded with the peculiar emphasis of one a little the worse for drink. "The guardian of my sanity is still the fair Beula. 'I went alone to a secret place, To find my lady fair. I didn't dare to show my face. 'Cos all the world was there.'" He drained the glass, "Is it true?"

"Is what true?"

"All the world has been to my secret place. Have they?"

"Have who?"

"THEY."

Beula felt tears behind her eyes, "The answer is No."

"None of them or all of them?"

"None of them."

"Or some of them?"

"One of them."

"Ah."

"Has Rowena been to my secret place?"

"That's different."

"It's not different."

"It is different. She's my wife."

Beula put a hand to her face.

"Look, not recently."

"Tell me one thing, Jeremy. If you'd never met Rowena, would you have thought seriously of me?"

"You?"

"Me. Me me ME."

He sat, back to her, stirring the drink round and round. When at last he spoke he sounded like an early transatlantic pilot radioing through a storm, "It's possible," he seemed to be saying, "But look at it this way, what chance would we have had?"

*

When Jeremy got to the parquedero, he found it unattended. The youth with the candid eyes had vanished so had the windscreen wipers, four hub caps and all the fuel in the tank plus the stopper. Help came with a flask of gasoline and stack of newspapers. The frail-looking gas pump attendant twisted a copy of *El Espectador* round and round to make a blind cone and plugged it into the tank. Then he spread out the other sheets and showed Jeremy how to use the print to blot the windshield.

29

It was a moonless night and there was thunder about. Beula couldn't tell if she should attach the windscreen wipers because of rain or if she was crying. She slammed her front door without locking it, did not check window locks or draw curtains, dragged up the five stairs to her bedroom and fell on the bed. For a long time she blotted her face with the sheet, knowing she was in for one of those nights that occur when you're single, relatively young, healthy and employed, that is to say with expectations. The hobgoblin has you by the throat and you doubt you can last the night. The ironhearted, the capable achieve suicide.

At the foot of the bed, Yuri, the larger cat, unsettled by the interruption, stretched.and with blurry eyes, went to Beula, planting paws on her shoulder. Sitting up, she scratched the cat's neck, smoothed his belly and pulled his tail, taking comfort from his warmth and vibrations, soothed by his furriness, his indifference to whether she married her heart's desire or remained an underdog till retirement.

Once the sobbing had eased she rose, put on a knitted dressing gown and bedsocks and made her way down to the living room to pace. Steno, the female cat, appeared, tail erect and mewing. Up to the orange sofa, back to the windowbox. At least I shan't get a headache. It's too bad for that. I was no more than a side dish. Tears started up again. Across the avocado carpet to the window box and back. Up to the wooden bottom step and back. For some reason her father's comments on her potcleaning began to resound: 'A big girl's blouse.' 'A cow handling a musket.' She pressed her face to the window. How many times? Seven hundred? Wrapping herself in a ruana, she settled in front of the window to wait for the dawn.

*

At ten minutes to seven Nolita let herself in, crossed the living room to leave her bag on the kitchen table then recrossed to bolt the front door. Seeing her employer in an armchair she stopped dead, "*Gesu Cristo*," What are you doing there? Waiting for *rateros*? You didn't even lock up. They could have broken in. Chloroformed you!"

As a rule Nolita's presence had a way of makings things seem less solid, especially matters of the heart. To see her scurrying around looking out aspirins, bringing in the milk, made the apartment come alive. But it didn't help Beula's fragile, overheated state, didn't disperse the deep sadness, the hopelessness. Since their trip to the north coast and the advance of an extra week's pay, Nolita had been wonderful. Whether Nolita would do the same if their position were reversed was not clear. Would she be leaving it up to me, Beula wondered, to concoct harmony out of confusion? Nolita gave her one long look, slapped her knees and burst into cackling.

"Love trouble is it?" Another gust of merriment, "Well," wiping an eye on her apron, "Maybe it's time to plunge. Otherwise you'll wind up like me. Beached." More cackling, looking down at Beula in lively interest, her broad, brown face crumpled in a mask of temporary gravity. She never came too close. Neither would she sit when invited, standing almost to attention, a square squat figure, hands under the heavily stained but laundered apron, reflecting that Beula's pallor and dark eyes reminded her of a painting in Doña Clara's house of the last scene of some opera.

"Come on senorita, have a good cry, *llore, llore.*"

Beula shook her head. "It's too bad for tears. I've come to the end of my life."

Nolita bent over to rearrange the ruana, "*Oiga,* you'll get dressed, put the elastic on your hair. The car'll show up at ten to eight. You'll rush down the path and get home after six."

"No, I'm paralyzed. Been clobbered by two or three words. They've taken meaning out of life. I can't face going to the office. Can't face coming home. What's the point of getting showered putting clothes on or getting made up? Don't tell me things will be the same. They'll never be the same," she waved the coffee cup away, "I've been dealt variations of the same old blow too many times. Told that I'm nice but not quite. What are some of the things I'm accused of?" her voice rose, 'Not a type to settle down with.' What did he say?" she shouted, "'Our relationship doesn't have an everyday texture.' Couldn't see how it could stand up to life on his salary." She looked up, eyes shining, "Translated that means I'm not provided for. He saw me as a fix, a chance to indulge those senses deadened by life with her. I don't exist as a person in my own right. I'm a service."

"It's Don Jeremy isn't it?"

Beula closed her eyes.

"Don Jeremy will never marry you senorita. Not that one. I could have warned you but I didn't like to. With a rich wife what does he need you for? *Mucha disfruta de Vd.* Of course the wife's carrying on with that waiter—the whole town knows. He lives two floors up from her dressmaker. After her fitting she pops upstairs to her fancy man. Severa's sister, Altagracia, works on the floor in between and I hear plenty about the goings on."

Beula reached over to the coffee tray, "Are there any more sugar crystals, Nolita?" She leant back in the orange armchair, both hands around the oversized coffee cup," Are you quite sure?"

"*Claro*, but I'm discreet. I won't swear to it."

"Do you know any more?"

"This I know. Before you came Don Jeremy was parading up and down here trying to lure your predecessor. She never took up the bait and though I never agreed with her on anything, she made sense in that direction. I never cared for him myself. But at least he's an improvement on his predecessor, Don Marmion, who had a different woman every night of the week, nurses, waitresses, prostitutes. One morning I saw a dancer sitting cross-legged like a brass idol. Jeremy is quieter and he has a nice smile."

Beula felt able to cry and Nolita grimly nodding, pottered off and came back with a pillow and clean towel.

"Just stay put. At eight o'clock I'll call Don Camber and tell them you're poorly." She took Beula's hand. Her fingers smelled of garlic and potato and Beula buried her nose in them.

"At some stage you felt as I do."

Nolita shook her head, "Not me, senorita."

"You never were in love?"

"Never," she asserted proudly, "I don't say I didn't have chances but I saw through it. One Sunday afternoon when I was working at the house of *senor el ministro*,. I'd just left mamita's graveside. There was a young fellow, not unlike the chino, waiting behind the flower stall. He followed me all the way back to my street. Never lingering and that showed respect. I got used to seeing him by the cemetery gate. Ay, he was good looking, thick, straight hair." She stretched, flexed her arms and pounded her ribs. "His eyes weren't black like mine. They were brown like *marrones* and they burned. I felt them burning into my back. I felt them when I got home at night. One evening just as I'd closed the gate he came out of the shadow and spoke to me. I knew he wasn't the sort to pull out a knife. He said he'd like to make my acquaintance and could he walk with me? Well, we walked and I knew then that if I wanted that man I could have had him. Not just as a lover but in matrimony."

"But you didn't."

"*Que va*! Of course I didn't."

"Didn't he appeal?"

"All men have some sort of appeal. Lift heavy things. Some have money. Even Don Camber has something. You see, senorita, I was forty years old. The young one of the family. Out of seven boys and five girls, eight are already dead. Offed in *La Violencia*, some in police raids, two in a busload by machete. Mamita and I had trouble identifying them, So I took charge of caring for mamita especially when her eyes failed and she couldn't see to sew."

Beula sat like a child waiting for mother to turn the page.

"For many years I looked after my mama. And now she's gone and my God I do miss here. There was nobody like mamita."

"Oh Nolita, what about the admirer?"

"I ask myself, senorita. What is life with a man? Do I want a man ordering me about? Do I want to be muchacha in my own house? If I didn't marry early and beget a lot of people to order me about, was I going to marry late and beget a few people who'd order me about? I wasn't going to risk being beaten." She folded her arms, "For years I thought Nolita had nothing. Now I know otherwise. My room. It's a decent size, better than the cupboard I had at the villa of senor el ministro. There's a coldwater pump in the yard and a sink. Nolita does without hot water. Two windows, stone floor, gas ring, electric outlet. Forty pesos a month towards charcoal. On damp nights when the clouds hang low I have a nip of something—aguardiente with lemon. I say my prayers.

"Oh I could have married that fellow. Young he was, younger than me. I expect he's dead by now, killed in prison or in a riot. I did look for him among a pile of dead but faces go black especially the battered ones. Once or twice he gazed at me in a funny way like he was looking for something. I suppose it must have been home comforts."

Beula drank the coffee in a series of sips and lay the cup carefully down, "Well if you're saying dismiss Don Jeremy what's the alternative?"

"If you want my honest opinion I think you should take Pablito," Nolita started one of whoops, throwing her head back, laughing in an uncontrolled, unladylike way.

"I can't afford him. You have him."

Nolita started skipping, "Years ago I could have had him free of charge. *Mira,* money, even old money isn't all roses. I've worked in two of the great houses around here. Houses where they keep four or five maids along with a major domo lording it over the wine steward, where the lady of the house stands like this," She drew herself up to her full height throwing her head back, "'*Muchacha,*' she'd say, '*Traigami la cartera.*' Bring me my handbag.

"I know the rich. Working in houses as I've done for thirty-eight years, I started out slaving for people who looked middle class but really were sub middle class. One family, the Perecitos who had me running here, running there, were hardly better off than my brother's family. I said to myself if I have to be a skivvy, I'll be a skivvy to the rich. Mind you, the rich are no more considerate than the poor and they don't pay better, but the leavings are good. I had my tinto at a table instead of on the back steps. Big flower gardens, tennis courts. I used to think Doña Clara's life was magic. I helped dress her daughter in a gold embroidered wedding gown. Hair all braided with lilies. I used to dream that one day some of that magic would rub off onto me. But it didn't then and it didn't later. Why? Because the magic's in me, not her. Took me quite a few years to figure that one out. The girl got fat, ugly even. Left sherry bottles under the mattress.

"The thing I noticed about Doña Clara's family was they were ordinary. I don't mean vulgar. They were no more vulgar than the poor.

What I mean is they were nothing special. Oh they could drive a car, ride a horse, one even took up gardening."

Sounds like me, Beula thought blowing her nose, except I can't do two out of three.

"...didn't have Doña Clara's voice. Mr. Lanchester used to call it, what was it? A plethora of choices. *Entonces* I said adios to the rich and started working for the foreigners. I didn't leave the rich because they were ordinary. I left because they made me feel I didn't exist especially when my arthritis started up.

"Don't think they didn't have worries. Not only did they have back-ache, they had bellyache and heartache. Doña Clara's niece nineteen years old. *Linda, linda.* Goes to the tenth floor of her father's office block in the middle of the night, gets the *sereno* to let her in, goes out on the terrace and jumps. For love apparently. The rich know something the poor don't know which is," she pulled at a hair on her chin, "you can be more desperate. I've watched them at their morning bridge and their after-tennis tea parties and you should see their faces. I know about these things.." She relaxed in a Stone Age smile, "Still, a few dollops of big money wouldn't break my heart. But I'm different."

30

It was with uncanny relief that Jeremy crossed his front porch, closed the glazed inner door and tiptoed across the circular hall to the study. He could not say why he was creeping about in his own house. What he did know was he did not want to ruffle the calm that had stolen over him. He stretched out on the hard chaise longue, legs apart in the corpse position, rolling his head from side to side. Presently his eyes followed the busy back-and-forth cleaning action of the housekeeper's son on the window sill. This changed to a half-circular motion which made him drowsy. Soon his eyes closed. He felt a car rug being laid over him and smoothed out. When he awoke the window cleaner had gone and Rowena was moving to and fro with a long gold cord.

His wife usually gave every sign of keeping attention in the present and outside self. On her 'altitude' days, however, attention reverted to self, her mind taking detours away from the present. Like yesterday at Mrs. Grapnel's coffee morning, trying to memorize her panto number while Mumtaz outlined techniques for the prevention of cake burglary at gamine benefits. And that same afternoon at panto rehearsal, wondering how exactly party cake is removed whole. Today was one of her good days. Her voice had returned. She had made a Dundee cake to surprise Jeremy. The new sculpted haircut had set off her looks in an impish, less answerable form, "Are you ready for tea now?" she asked, wrinkling her eyes.

He propped himself up on the bolster, "Don't think so, darling. No, no cake, well perhaps a teeny wedge. To tell the truth I feel a bit dragged out. What have we got tonight?"

"Food drive for the gamines," Rowena held tight to the teapot as the golden liquid swirled around in the Royal Doulton.

"Ah yes, goodie. We needn't get there till nine."

She drank tea thirstily, "Did you get the mini back?"

"'Course I did, darling, she's in the garage."

"Running OK?"

"Think so."

"You sound unsure," She lifted the teapot again and rocked it back and forth without taking her eyes from him.

"I must confess she's missing hub caps and petrol tank cap. But I managed to fit a spare set of windscreen wipers I found in the glove compartment."

"You mean the garage lifted them?"

"Darling, did I say that?"

"Well then who?"

"Search me."

"Where did you park?"

"Dropped off a package at the Salvador."

"They must have moved awfully fast."

"I was parked miles from the barrier."

"Why go in so deep for God's sake?"

"Full up."

"It isn't usually at that time."

"Darling, would you mind awfully asking them to pour me a cognac soda? No ice. It's my first today. Didn't even have beer at lunch. Press the tit. By the way how was rehearsal?"

"That's tomorrow."

"Ah."

"Although I could have done with the mini today. I can't face any more rides with Mumtaz. You know what her hill starts are like."

Jeremy smiled to himself. He was starting to feel at ease at home for the first time in months, "You know this cake's not at all bad," he leant over, cupping his hand over her elbow, "In whatever you do, darling, you excel." He lay back. Presently he said, "I don't need a drink after all. I'm starting to wind down. Perhaps I'll go up and have a warm bath and a rest. You can join me later if you feel like it." She looked up quickly without showing surprise.

Later, in a candlewick bathrobe, Jeremy held his wife in his arms, "I'm glad you did join me, darling," he murmured, pressing back a stray tendril of hair, "I wasn't sure you would. Was afraid you might be cutting out a camisole for Dulcinea. But now that you're here I want to tell you something. Do you know that you look beautiful? Very beautiful."

"Sounds American."

"Beautiful then," he put a hand over her shoulder and gently stroked her spine.

She turned on her back and lay against his hand, one arm under her head, gray eyes darting back and forth. She'd put on a frilly playgown of pink and blue pergale. When she turned to him, her look took him back to their courtship days at Oxford. Slowly she began rotating her right foot and, reading the signal, he rolled over and held her close. They kissed and he was back in her father's conservatory with the scent of gardenia, the night they got engaged. He tried to remember the shape of the glasshouse. Was it rectangular? No, it had odd corners. Was it a trapezium? No it had no acute angles. That was the night he felt his feet on the right track. Oh the buoyancy of those glad days, trips to the West

End, driving along back lanes, dawns in the summerhouse wrapped in old blankets, the looking ahead to even better times. Days when the chinking of ice in the bucket, the feel of a really soft pair of leather shoes, opened up vistas of sensory adventure. Absently, he began stroking her spine again. She writhed for a moment, then closed her eyes and was still.

"It's no good," she smoothed the playgown, "You mustn't rub. Remember our talk about planes of sensation and our conclusion. You surely must have taken in that Rubbing and Scrubbing never leads to the Next Plane. If anything it puts me on the plane below. You were going to try for the right touch, remember? I believe you could if you thought about it but you don't think. Why not caress instead of rub? And please bear in mind that I can't stand being touched on my neck or my buttocks and certainly not on my abdomen. I can't endure it. You seem to have blacked out all the stages we discussed. You promised to do the steps in order. Surely you took that in? Go from lips to breast and proceed from there. You can't start with spine and go on to thighs and back to stomach."

Jeremy smiled and nodded. No matter. He would make it work The order of ascending zones of erogeny made sense to him and he should have known better than to wander into by-lanes. She smelled delicious and somehow he'd work it out. Small overtures, small and enduring, no darting back and forth. Achieve the end phenomenon of one zone, move up the scale. Never err by moving too fast or idling too long in between zones. How is one to know when to move on? Should he clamber on while they kissed? Better not. Still, the kissing felt good, better than anything since their arrival sixteen months ago. Keeping his cool, he worked through one zone and hesitantly entered the next. Moving his head round in slow motion he said in her ear, "Have you inserted any lubricant?"

"Yes I have," she whispered, "also the diaphagm. In case any has fallen out, I'll insert a little more." She stretched out a languid hand to the white tube behind the bolster and massaged her parts carefully with it, then added, "Here's some for you."

"I haven't yet removed my underpants."

"Please try to avoid unsettling everything. If you keep gathering up the bedclothes like this can you imagine what it does to my nerves? I can't cope with all the flapping about. I think it submerges the libido."

"I love you, Rowena."

She waited for him to settle then said, "I dream of coalescing in a sensual silence." After a moment she added, "But your hands are stone cold."

They lay together, perfectly still. He waited for her to give him a go-ahead and an Are you ready? before bestirring himself.

"Would you like me to smear some on you?"

"Ooh that's cold. But it's all right. Now are you ready?"

"Wait a minute. Yes. Go ahead."

"No," he rolled over to his side, "I was all right a second ago."

"You've gone down like an inner tube."

"Don't say that please. Just keep kissing and caressing me."

"It's disheartening. As though you're playing a game. Once I get excited you want to quit the playing field. At a deeper level I believe you're dead set against my having any gratification."

"Rowena you know that's not true."

"Yes it damn well is. The minute I feel stirrings you back off. But when your need arises it must be attended to. Never mind what kind of mood I'm in. You must think that just because I'm at home I'm available. Well I'm not. If you want to make a rendezvous you should allow at least forty-eight hours notice."

"Rowena, listen to me. Have you got an image? What about the nineteen-year old Berber prostitute, what was his name, Abdeslam?"

"I never knew him as Abdeslam. It was always Rachid.

"Have you got Rachid focused?'

"I've worn that one out."

"The wife of the camel driver?"

"I had that last time. What you don't realize is it's got to be naughty."

"Dear me. Why don't we try a gang bang with the Harlem Globetrotters?

She turned on her back again, "I have these images because I'm never sure where your attention is. You touch me with the sole idea of giving yourself pleasure. The idea of me as myself never enters your head."

"How can you think anything as pitiless as that."

"Just now you went to step three without making sure I got my end result on step two."

"How am I to know for sure where you are?"

"You're always sounding off about knowingness. You just have to Know that's all. Tune into me for Christ's sake. To me."

"I believe I'm already tuned into you. You know how much I care don't you? And I believe, I hope, you care about me."

"Yes Jeremy. I care."

"Would you say you find me irresistible?"

"Isn't that the same thing?"

"Then say it."

"I do find you irresistible."

"Ah that's better. Better better better. I'm getting close. Are you ready?"

"I might be."

He rolled over, hovered over her, kissing her hair and ear, "No," he sighed, "As you were."

"Why does this have to happen to us? Most couples have an adequate sex life, at least halfway decent."

"Who, for instance?"

"Here we're not on those terms."

"Mumtaz doesn't confide about Hot Flash's performance. His knee-jerk reaction. And Camber and Fleur must be up the creek if she's absent three months after a D. and C. What about our friends at home? Does marital sex come up at dinner parties?"

"My cousin Aurora says that after the third child she ran into the dryzie dries."

"I mean those who have."

Night had fallen and the clock radio set up a loud buzzing.

"I bet that office floozy gets her share," Rowena commented, "that Beula Waterhole. By all accounts she's been had by everyone in sight, including Grapnel. Those black stockings and tiny little dresses must clue them in on her needs."

Jeremy's heart leapt as he lay staring at the embossed ceiling while Rowena expressed doubts of sexual incompatibility. Suddenly she sat up in the darkness and thumped the clock radio, crying out, "We just don't have the chemistry."

"My dear girl, you know we've had some good goes. What about Madeira, what about Basingstoke? Here, let me give you a bit of a diddle and then you'll feel all right. I'm Rachid and I just climbed over the wall. Come now, kiss me." After a minute or two he said, "Spread a little of the jelly on me. Be careful, my state's fragile. Are we ready to shoot?" Then he added, "How does it feel?"

"Not too bad."

"Here we go."

Later he rolled onto his back, and lay in the crook of her armpit collecting himself. After a minute or two he turned to face her, "Did it hurt darling. Tell the truth."

"Did it hurt you?"

"Didn't get grazed this time. I'm asking about you, darling. Did you enjoy it, but really? Did you fly?"

"Well…"

"Didn't hurt, though?"

"Only slightly."

"We didn't use enough lube. Let me come to the rescue. Relax and above all don't try. Forget about time. I don't have to collect the mad parson till eight forty-five."

31

"My orders are to let no one in." Nolita's voice through the closed door was muffled but Phuff thought he detected an insubordinate lilt.

"Look Nolita," he shouted through the letter box, "You have no choice but to let me in. This is no social call. I represent her employer. If I report to His Excellency that I'm denied entry she may be recalled to London by the next plane and you might find yourself on the bread line."

"Bread line!" was the response, "Not Nolita who cleans without floor polisher or even vacuum cleaner. Who knows risotto, quiche, frittata. Very few muchachas cook these days and if they do they make it taste so nobody wants to eat in."

"For the sake of the senorita, open the door? If you don't she stands to lose her job."

Nolita opened to the extent of the safety catch, "They can't terminate for three days absence without a medical certificate."

"You seem to have read the last but one executive directive."

"Transfer only happened once in my memory," Nolita shouted through the opening, "Senorita Gumm who caught syphilis from an insurance adjuster. Even if the senorita is transferred I have choices. Apart from being a cook I have my own room."

"Perhaps we could discuss this over a cup of espresso?"

"What is there to discuss? My orders are to let no one in."

"Just a short talk and I'll give you a lift home."

There was more shuffling before Nolita unlocked the door. Avoiding her eye and missing the new spectacles, Phuff clumped up the hall stairs. Once inside the apartment, he looked around the living room, "Where is she?"

"In her bedroom."

He climbed the five stairs and after a moment's hesitation gave an impalpable knock, "Beula, this is Camber Phuff. I've come to investigate the reason for your absence Monday, Tuesday and Wednesday. And no medical certificate."

Silence.

"Can you hear me Beula? Have you contacted a doctor?" He knocked louder, "H.E. requires an explanation." Something rustled within. He bent down and put his red ear to the keyhole. The door opened a fraction for Steno, the leaner cat, to strut out, and closed again.

"You realize that this sort of thing will go on your personnel report under some heading like Deviant Behavior? Beula, do you really look forward to spending your declining years in the lowest of grades? Picture yourself an older lady with young girls getting promoted over you." To Nolita, "Is there a key to this door?"

"Locks from the inside if you turn the knob."

"Beula I know about Bradstein. I met him and his boy-friend at badminton. I do commiserate. But let's be objective. The feller was out of range." He gave a half-chuckle, half-snort, "I must say, you do seem to have the luck. In straightforward circumstances he might have been the answer but the truth is you'd be barking up the wrong tree, no matter how hard you worked on him."

At that the bedroom door shot open and the *fata morgana* appeared, holding a book. Camber was surprised to see her fully dressed and made up as for a costume party in a silver bolero, sequinned knee breeches and heavy jade earrings. Pale and intense, she stood framed in the doorway for fully a minute, as though about to speak and Camber should not.

"Worked hard on him?" Beula said in a low voice, "Worked hard on him indeed. You don't seem to have grasped the fact that I could engage in a relationship which is not...defined by ah narrow self-interest. I may seem to you to be a bitch in heat but I knew what kind of tree Bradstein was," her voice rose, "You might ponder the fact that the one male among my acquaintances here, who has no...testicular interest in me, is the only one to make me feel I'm...I'm someone." She gripped the balustrade, looking as though she had not slept for three nights. Her makeup was patchy and caked. Globs of mascara clung to her eyelids. There was a terrible seriousness about her. "You were advising me from your standpoint," she shrieked, "What do you know about my standpoint?"

"Well, Beula, do you know about it?" Camber turned away from her and paced the narrow landing.

"I suppose," she fiddled with a sequin, "you think your advice is of value. Thanks for your concern that I might wind up an ancient grade 3 because I missed the glorious marriage." The setting sun illuminated her breeches making Phuff shield his eyes. "But there'll be no more hiding my light under a bushel to please the likes of the boys network." She held up a hand for silence, "Because prostituting myself in marriage is no better than prostituting myself in a job. Both are relics of what patriarchy sees as my role. Slave at the workbench, slave in the bedroom." She descended the five stairs and knocked at the kitchen door. When Nolita opened, Beula shook a finger at Phuff, "No more Madeira. Scotch only"

Phuff cleared his throat, "Let's try to put patriarchy's role on the back burner."

"It won't sit. Any time the Pat Ice gets driven out in times of war, it waits for the dust to settle and then it slithers back Holds meetings to set trends. Saw to it that at puberty Beula got classified as a hole. Aitch Oh El Ee!"

Head shaking, Phuff took the whisky glass.

Beula puckered one side of her face, "A HOLE. My father called it Jam Tart. Wears high heels and high skirts. Worries. Picks up the falling glass."

Phuff frowning, peered at the pale gold of his drink, "I hope you won't entirely renounce the idea of wedlock."

"Bradstein said something else," she muttered. "About America where…"

"Tell you what, Beula, I'm having chipolatas tonight. No, not chipolatas. Potato pancakes. What would you say to potato pancakes and stewed apples?"

"…nobody gives a damn where you start out."

"Have you thought of registering with a marriage bureau?"

She began laughing in a disturbed way.

"Don't you have a hanky?"

"I'm fed up with sexual kindness."

"May I know what that means?"

"It's," she blotted her eyelid with the edge of an envelope, "Deference to a hidden purpose." She bent down and lifted a small spider dangling inside her knee breeches and swung the thread behind the arm of the chair. Her drink lay untouched. She put her hand in the glass and took out some ice, "I don't need just one more…lover." She rubbed the ice cube against her forehead, "All right," she sighed without looking up, "Collect me this evening if you must and drive me up to your place for potato pancakes. Under my rules."

Phuff frowned, "My dear, I don't want to see you fall apart," He turned over the book she'd thrown down, "The Times of Dickens."

32

*S*tretched out in the back of the chauffeur-driven Lagonda zooming along the autopista Jeremy, for the first time since Don Renardo's assassination a month earlier, counted himself almost in shape. He had endeavored to eat not what he fancied but what was right, placating a stomach that, bubbling like a geyser, cooked up methane and hydrogen sulphide vapor that seeped through the cracks. Take that and that, it seemed to say as he sat long and late at a dinner party. Oh the pain, the strain, the fight to retain. He'd begun fasting one whole day a week and excepting the odd twinge of acidity, the hystelitica did seem in recession. Stomach apart, goblins still sat in troughs in his shoulders. Still he thanked Osiris that the Black Velvet he'd had to down at Don Fedoro's reception last night had not left him so blotto he couldn't identify his own car.

He had been counting blessings. Arriving at a new post is rebirth. Goodbye Piccadilly, farewell to fumbling in a vandalized telephone kiosk, tata to the coffee queue in that slimy cafeteria where your table never gets wiped. Hello to the Third World where the DC3 taxis up to

147

the one-building airport, the admin officer greets you as if he has all day, where your arrival is the event of the month in New Atlanta, land of the poolside lunch, girlie bar, ironed pyjama. Believing the present situation will endure is a trap.

Lolling back on gray alpaca cushions, trees and shrubbery rushing past, he felt remote from the delivery. He'd checked documents and Emergency Envelopes 1 & 2, praying Fedoro would be in a better mood than during last night's soft soap and fleshpot banter. He's finding it hard to forgive me, Jeremy thought, for upstaging him with Her. Well, since Octavio's fiesta I've got nothing to hide.

At the airport turnoff, Jeremy told the driver to proceed to the VIP lounge. Without changing down Jorge raced into the terminal lane and swung the car round in a christiana type stop, spraying the car in a shower of shingle. The egg-shaped Jorge waddled up the three shallow steps to the VIP lounge then reappeared.

"Don Amo has left word that Don Fedoro will be at the freight depot, sir."

At the freight depot Jeremy was met by two guards, Gilberto and Enrico who explained that due to flooding the consignment was stored at Hangar Six, not Hangar One as on the manifest.

"Where is Don Fedoro?"

"He will be at Hangar Six."

"And how do I get there?"

"Drive to the edge of the runway, turn left and proceed a quarter of a mile. The road is unlighted due to power failure."

At the entrance to Hangar Six Jeremy drove into a barrier, alerting the guard who straightening his helmet, rose, lifted his weapon and stood to attention as Jeremy flashed the import license. Not glancing at the document the guard stated that entry was barred to any civilian.

"I am a close associate of Don Fedoro."

"Those are not my orders."

"Whose orders are they?"

"Lieutenant Jimenez, sir."

"Please tell the lieutenant that I am the commission rep."

"I cannot let you pass.'"

Jeremy put his briefcase between his knees and drew out Emergency Envelope No. 1. The guard peeped inside, counted the money and lifted the pole. At the reception desk, Jeremy tapped on the glass. A clerk slid it open and grunted, "*Que desea?*"

"Where's the shipment?"

"What shipment?"

Jeremy produced the import license. The clerk flipped through it with impatience, "Senor Jooning, you cannot enter the hangar. This is a copy."

"Tell Dr. Foudroya I have arrived."

"The clerk did not react to the name. "These telephones are out of order," he mumbled, returning to his study of 'The Faerie Queen.'

Jeremy brought out Emergency Envelope No. 2. "Is Don Amo's telephone working?" he asked.

The clerk, pocketing the envelope, carefully pressed down the dog-eared page he was studying and closed the book The corridor smelt of whisky. A policeman at a sink poured scotch through cheesecloth into a bowl.

"One third of the shipment has been collected by trucks Hilda and Kathleen," the clerk announced, "The remainder may not be seen by anyone who does not hold the original of the import license."

Jeremy rapped on the desk.

"There is a private telephone you may try," the clerk added, "At the foot of the spiral staircase take the door to the right," he pointed to a stairwell beyond the sink.

Jeremy descended the narrow, dimly-lit stair. At the foot he came to two doors, one was a closet. He opened the other door and entered. It snapped shut. An accordion grille unfolding in front of the door made a loud clatter. He was in a lift that shot him to the sub-basement. Finding himself in pitch black, he felt along the wall until he tripped on a pile of cardboard boxes. With a click the lift doors closed and the conveyance returned to point of origin. Jeremy pressed the button repeatedly but nothing happened. The cellar was unheated and as his eyes grew used to the dark, Jeremy found himself in a cell ten feet by ten feet, a pile of packing cases in one corner and what looked like boxes of ammunition in the other.

*

"Let me get this straight." The number one set his pillow against the bedhead, "Jooning went into Hangar Six and never came out."

"That is correct, sir." Phuff's voice crackled over the wire.

"Grapnel, on the edge of the bed, pulled at his pyjama cord, "Was Fedoro at the airport?"

"His presence was confirmed by Don Gilberto."

"I've never heard of Don Glberto."

"A number four, sir."

The STD reddened round the chin, "I hear Fedoro holds some sort of personal grudge against Jooning."

"Speaking off the record, sir, there was a big to-do about who should dance with a certain lady at Don Octavio's fiesta."

"Who was it who wanted to dance with the lady besides Fedoro? Well, was it Jooning? I said was it Jooning?"

"I'm told Fedoro felt unable to finish his dance with the lady."

"Tell me this. Was Fedoro upset?"

"On the whole, sir, I would say so."

"Very or exceedingly?"

"Well, I suppose the latter."

"Am I to conclude that Fedoro would endanger the delivery for the favors of some bit of skirt?" The STD scratched the back of his neck then gave a groan for Phuff to continue.

"If it's any consolation, sir, I did get some sort of lead."

"About Fedoro and the typist?"

"No sir, an anonymous phone call was relayed to the effect that the Urban Revolutionary Centrists claim responsibility for Jooning's capture."

"Never heard of them."

"Twenty two million was the figure quoted."

"How much is that in sterling?"

"Seven hundred and thirty nine thousand, five hundred and sixty, give or take."

Grapnel, bent over, head in hands.

"It's my feeling, Sir, that the Centrists would never make a preposterous offer like that if all they had to hand over were remains."

"How is Rowena taking it?"

"Sedated. It was she who received the demand."

"What's her father worth would you say? Roughly speaking."

"I have no access to knowledge of that kind. I did, however, read about G.J. Stilus's nomination to head of personnel. I'm told it's a brother of Rowena's."

*

Remedios sat on the paper-strewn carpet, leaning against Beula's sofa. Yuri, the larger cat, rose from the arm of the sofa and pawed her shoulder, "You may want me to scratch you, fatso," she said, turning from the cat's honeyed gaze, "But don't you feel free to scratch me." As Yuri carefully transferred from shoulder to lap, she felt under his belly, "This one's putting on tonnage."

Nolita placed Beula's Thai coffee pot on the sideboard, "Nothing's too good for those cats."

"I saw the senorita leave for work," Remedios said, taking the cup of espresso, "Red rings round the eyes."

"Anxiety. Don Camber said he was worried about her the night he drove me home, well not quite home—it would be just my luck to see one of my sister's kids as I get out of the car."

"What's the anxiety for?"

"A kidnapping. One of her bosses. Don Jeremy."

"What's he look like?"

Nolita firm against the sideboard, chewed thoughtfully, "Thin pointed eyebrows, scar under one eye. Ears like the devil."

"Green eyes?"

"Like stuffed olives.."

"I've seen him. I've seen him!"

"Not here you haven't."

"One morning at five o'clock, I open my door to let in some air and I see this stupendous gringo flat against the wall. Like a lizard. First off I thought it was the car dealer. A real Romeo, hardly breathing. In running shorts. I look again and phttt he's gone. Gone without moving. I saw the scar. I saw the devil's ears. He could have just crept down the stairs. From this apartment."

Nolita remained still, a bespectacled Chibcha statue.

"I mean," Remedios went on, "If she was thrown over by Green-Eyes I can certainly feel for her. I wish he'd been visiting me till five in the morning. Does he who's missing look like a movie star?"

Nolita took two mints out of the pocket of her stained but laundered overall, popped one in her mouth and handed the other to Remedios, "There are no movie stars in that delegation. Just a lot of clerks overfed and underworked telling each other to 'press the tit.' I doubt the senorita still sees the golden band as a cure-all because I haven't heard the word Marriage lately. Still she did come out with something the other morning. 'Nolita,' she says over her oatmeal, 'I've got nobody.' She still has her mother but this mother, where is she?"

"Like you, she has nobody."

"No I've got somebody. I have me."

*

"Who wants me? Charlotte take the plum out of your mouth. Personnel London! Why in God's name didn't you say? Gil Stilus? Hello,Gil. I've been trying to get you all day. Yes things are at last moving along. Through a local employee, Juan Minuto, we are in negotiation with the Centrists and, although I say it myself, there is progress. By careful reasoning, tough talk and endless patience we've got the URC down to the absurd sum of twenty five thousand pounds. Well, Gil, it wasn't easy. The dilemma is this. Is he alive or isn't he? If he's alive twenty five grand is a drop in the bucket.

"Look here, Gil, the money has to change hands soonest. The sum could be advanced out of public funds but the paperwork might take two weeks and we don't want to endanger Jeremy. I wondered if an approach might be made for your father to consider bridging the gap...? In the form of a loan in pesos...? Repaid at interest to be sure...Decision to be made today, Gil. No later than 1600 hours our time."

*

Three days later Rowena popped a head round the door, "Shall I tell them to bring you up some soup?"

"Fine darling. Press the tit. I won't be getting up this afternoon. Just want to laze around and try to read." Jeremy, hollow eyed, adjusted the pillows under his knees.

The telephone rang. Rowena leant across Jeremy to grab it, "Yes he's actually out...Here at home! Well, very shaky, can't stand up... Dehydration not acute. There was a filthy sump and he drank from that. Well what about the advance? They won't allow you to recoup it? Who won't? Why not? HMG does not advance monies for...What did you say? Pranks? Who said that?...Well Daddy I don't know what to think." She handed the telephone to Jeremy.

"Hello Sydney. I'm getting there...Pranks? Well there may be something to that. One moment I'm looking for a telephone. Next thing I'm in a dungeon. Tried sleeping on a pile of boxes but it was so damp I had to keep on the move. After a bit I lost track of time. Gracias, just leave it there.. HMG won't...reimburse did you say? I'm terribly sorry but I feel powerless. They can take it out of salary until 2010, I suppose. I said I'm sorry. Sydney, I'll say it again. Here's your father, Rowena."

"Daddy, please. This isn't so much of a sum these days. He's back for God's sake...Yes he is taking it seriously. So you started work at fifteen! How can it be our fault? Have I asked you for a bean? Recently? Yes I KNOW Excessive Financing Depletes Initiative...Daddy, I beg of you...You've never once seen me grovel...Hello, hello." She dropped the phone on the floor and threw herself across the bed.

Jeremy leant over to smooth her hair, "It's all right."

"He's cancelling his visit."

"It's not serious."

"He never rants. I tell you he's going to cut us out."

"Why would he?."

"Feels he's been made a laughing stock. Claims someone had it in for you."

Jeremy slowly sat up.

"Do you know anyone who might have wanted to play that sort of trick?"

Jeremy bit his lip. Thrust in penile penitentia by some oligarch's dementia, he said to himself.

"You know don't you?"

"Know what?"

"You're not telling. And for some reason I don't believe it's out of fear of being sent home. Come on, out with it."

"Ultima ultima experiencia," he muttered.

33

"And so," intoned the Reverend Davison Newdoch, "in our conviction that we alone have sovereignty over our planet, that humankind is the only species that counts, we ignore God's laws. Let us consider Isaiah l, verses ll to l6.

> *'Your countless sacrifices, what are they to me?'*
> *says the Lord, 'I am sated with the whole offerings*
> *of rams and the fat of buffaloes. I have no desire for*
> *the blood of bulls of sheep and he-goats...There is*
> *blood on your hands, wash yourselves and be clean.*
> *Put the evil of your deeds, away out of my sight.'*

"Now for our closing hymn, number 329 To Dust Shall We return."

Beula got slowly to her feet. Between the coiffures of Charlotte and the Poison Dwarf she could see part of Jeremy's overshorn head, hunched over the pump organ. That Rowena was not in church was not unusual. Born a Catholic, she put in a token appearance, standing for hymns, not singing. Beula's boyish treble rose up from the back of the knave, causing one or two heads to turn. After the hymn Jeremy appeared at the front pew holding the offertory plate. She watched him from between two columns. As he paused at the end of the row she saw how skeletal his face had become. Three days and nights in darkness without fresh water and twenty five thousand gone to a group who never sequestered him. Now the story around the office of an apology from the Banco for the 'unaccountable lapse.'

After the postlude the parson, resplendent in gold-embroidered robes of cream and clover cretonne, took up the cross and walked with great dignity in a recessional. The expatriate congregation rose and looked around, nodding to acquaintances. Older matrons clogged the north door to shake hands with the parson whose last service it was. If, as was whispered, he had been asked to step down, this was not apparent from the congratulatory posture of the crowd surrounding him, foretelling a joyous and gratifying retirement.

The mad parson was a funny fellow, Beula decided, seeing him extend both hands to the flock, paying heed to the gibblegabble, not engrossed exactly and wearing a look of alcoholic intensity. It had been alleged by the trustee who wrote the incriminating letter that as well as liking his pint he liked little boys. But those who worked with him knew that his provision of food, comfort and shelter to hundreds of gamines was nothing if not high-minded. Beula found the post-sermon socializing a trial, the expatriates who met every other night chatting as if they hadn't seen each other for months. She pushed back her cuticles and had just made up her mind to leave when she felt a tug at her sleeve: the Poison Dwarf in a purple mini-dress, antipathy suspended in too warm a greeting.

"Wasn't that sermon ridiculous," commented the PD, "He never has had his biblical references straight. I always knew he was bent." She chuckled, "I say you do look most awfully tired. You'd better go and get yourself a nice hot cup of tea. I'd get it for you except I've got to rush."

Beula gathered up her ruana and moved to the end of the pew. Elna followed, "Have you heard the latest?" she whispered, "Rowena's left

Jeremy. Yes! Packed her bags and flown out. They're trying to keep it quiet at the office! He took me out last night to the Salvador Grille. Well," her eyes glowed, "over our second bottle of Vieux Ceps, he gave out that Rowena can't stomach the prospect of a London posting, life in a flat in Maida Vale, selling pantyhose at Harrods. On top of that her father wants Jeremy to repay every penny of the twenty five grand before the end of the year. Rowena has hardly spoken to him except to object to his frailty," Elna laughed lightly, "After he got most of it off his chest we had a divine evening."

"Where did she get to?" Beula asked in flat tones.

"Talked of staying at her father's place in Lucerne. But she'll bloody soon get tired of that. Anyway, I'm to wait for him so I'll leave you." In a cloud of *Ma Manie* the PD stumped up the aisle. Beula bent down to replace a hassock on its hook and unsteadily made her way to the vestibule. No sign of Jeremy. Or Elna. At the north door she spotted a wisp of purple and followed as it whirled down the spiral stairs to the conservatory where the ration of imported congress tart was fast disappearing. On tiptoe among the huddles of coffee drinkers, something told her to look no further. Those remaining were beginning to leave for the Reverend Newdoch's farewell at the British Embassy.

At the top of the stairway leading to the toilets she met the parson, lumpy and disgruntled, coming down. Timidly, she put out a hand, "I-I know you probably don't have a second, but I just wanted to wish you all the best and...and to thank you for the sermon." To her surprise he took her hand and held it. His hand felt cold and large.

"I'm glad you liked it," he replied, raising his chin, "There's always the tendency among congregants to dismiss the sermon as having no relevance to them. That emboldened me to put together today's offering out of the meager resources of the local library. It took me three weeks because the subject of people and Creation rarely gets an airing. The substance and rendition, even though I say it myself, came over fairly well. You're the only one who's even mentioned it." Talking, he grew animated and younger looking. She began to see the handsome blade inside the crumbling exterior.

Fingering his surplice shyly as the parson told how gold braids are glued onto the bands, Beula turned to find Jeremy had slipped between them. Her heart did not turn over but did go out to him, seeing the want and misery in his eyes as he listened to the churchman. They stood at the top of the stairway, a temporal company of three, breathing in conviviality. After a while, in the absence of any more nodding, Reverend Newdoch asked Jeremy about his condition. Did it still hurt him to breathe?

"Well it doesn't padre, thanks be to God, but it does hurt to laugh so don't tell us the one about the bishop's organ."

Abruptly Beula turned to the parson and said, "I want to get married."

Jeremy held his chest in embarrassment. The parson was quiet for a minute, then said, "I'd be glad to officiate my dear, if you have someone in mind."

At that Jeremy putting on an Yves Montand voice said, "Would I be your sort of candidate?"

After the parson had left Jeremy took Beula's hand, "I've kept out any hint of divorce around the office. I haven't yet told Grapnel. But what I want to say is this. When all the commotion's over, will you, won't you consider marrying me?"

*

From that moment Beula felt raised and remote from everyday annoyance. She saw Elna get into Jeremy's car, was conscious of delays at the car park exit, heavy traffic along the autopista. She clearly remembered the light turning green as a pick-up truck, driver high in his cab, crossed her path denting her right wing. At very far remove, she heard the altercation.

She was to be Married. To the man she loved. God, wasn't that the way things worked out? Darling, she had said, never having the used the word before, how does being Catholic fit in with divorce? With his funny crenellated grin Jeremy had told her not to worry her head, that it was all to be worked out on the basis of incompatibility. That in eight weeks time his tour is over and it's back to London. Not for long because Personnel can be decent at times.

"How long does a divorce take?"

"Oh, a couple of months. Rowena's gone to the house in Liss, which is in her name, I'm afraid. So I'm left with a funny little flat in Maida Vale."

Maida Vale. She'd begun to get a look at the kaleidoscope.

"But you know, darling," Jeremy added, "our discretion has now got to be absolute."

34

They got engaged at the Chinese restaurant on Avenida Dos Robales, a high-class operation in an opulent villa. Jeremy had obtained an emerald through a contact who knew a mine-worker who had somehow assembled a cache. The uncut stone had been rushed to another contact for cutting and to a third house for setting. Jeremy was not altogether satisfied with the final price and Beula thought the stone had got pared down. Yet, the gem fragment seemed to have magical properties. Held low in front of a window it revealed a cloud forest, and, under a light bulb, Wells Cathedral.

Beula had a new sensation. Happiness. Gratefully she typed the draft agenda for the Operation Hilda vesting, paying extra attention to format and terminology. Her social life was shifting in subtle ways. Every courtesy of the heretofore remained, but attendant on her inner euphoria came respect, which, plus a new air of unassailability, reinforced allure. Though not a soul had been let in on the secret, more doors opened. At a recent dinner party, seven men out of the ten present had got to their feet when she rose to excuse herself. Admirers had varying reactions. Pablito, seeing no reason to end the *amorio*, had, with a slow smile, swept aside Nolita's deflections, turning up as usual for the Monday evening ping pong. He was allowed a waiting time of one hour and if the senorita happened to return, was granted three games and one drink with no leave to change clothes.

Jeremy and Beula met with great discretion four times a week. On Wednesday evenings straight from work Beula drove up to Phuff's chalet for high tea, a welcome counterpoise to the celebrated moments with Jeremy. Elbows on Phuff's white damask tablecloth, she would smile to herself recalling Jeremy's witticisms about the early morning transports. Equally, in Jeremy's arms, she more than once dreamt of Phuff's brown toast and welsh rarebit made with beer. At the end of the nearly vertical lane she'd struggle out of the mini feeling on top of the world.

With Phuff in suedette slippers shouting greetings from the kitchen, Beula sat down to tea-cosy on trivet, sauted potatoes in casserole, celery in porcelain jar, half a Brie. The previous Wednesday they finished a two pound Christmas pudding and a quart of Bird's custard. Phuff had not so much as placed a hand on her arm. Neither had he showed signs of caring whether she changed the rules even after half a bottle of Madeira. Grapnel was not to know about Jeremy or Camber. Camber was not to know about Jeremy, but Jeremy knew about Camber. Jeremy had written off Pablito and Pablito suspected Jeremy.

Beula surrendered to bliss, quite as she had pictured. Jeremy driving them to his villa. after nightfall, her giggling from the floor of her own car. She sneaking out before his maid came on duty, over pearly lawns, across cobbles to the side lane, beating Nolita to her door. Nolita packing olive pastries and chirimoya to nibble on the Friday afternoon drive down to Orillas del Oro, at the foot of the mountain. Jeremy arriving earlier would have arranged for Beula to join his party for dinner. Sustained by visions of certainty, the pleasures of the social round erupted into something headier. A margarita became an elixir. Once the cup had drained the need would not return. She felt indestructible.

35

A few days later, putting order into the stationery cupboard, Beula noticed her colleague, head in hands. Luisito had been in with coffee and the PD hadn't even bothered to look up.

"Elna," Beula called, "Coffee's getting cold." She squeezed her colleague's shoulder, "Are you feeling all right?"

Elna's eyes were unbecomingly swollen, "Leave me alone." Convulsed in sobs, she struggled out of the typing chair and tore down the corridor.

Beula sat for a moment then lifted the telephone, saying in a baritone, "Is that you Phyllis?"

"Yes Harry, what can I do for you?"

"I'm concerned about PD. I wondered if the organist knew why?"

"I expect because she didn't get her promotion to second soprano."

"Oh is that all?"

"Well the organist gave her quite a talking to. Apparently she's to blame for the C flat legato. Now Harry, don't forget to prepare the minutes of the meeting." (Translation: the usual arrangement stands.)

As Beula resumed stacking up reams of xerox paper, sheds began moving into the stationery cupboard. Slight, hazy, growing solid, Mrs. Brownbill's ·asbestos full of holes, Mrs. Waterman's plywood tiled, Buggerlug's newly creosoted, all hovered between the shelves. As she scooped stray paperclips into a tin box, the conflict gradually identified itself. Her situation required extreme caution yet there was this yearning to bring matters out into the open.

Towards the end of the afternoon she lifted the intercom and dialled the STD's number, "This is Beula Kettlehole. I wonder, could you spare me a moment?"

Grapnel was writing when she opened the door. She sat in the nearest hard chair, covering her knees. At length he looked up, "Well Beula, what can I do for you?"

"You'll remember, Mr. Grapnel, that some time ago you asked if I had typed Draft Two of the contract. After mulling the matter over I've decided to make a clean breast of it," she lay a hand on the desk, "Mr. Grapnel, it was I not Elna who brought in the term 'cultural loan' to try to make sense of the sentence."

In the dead silence that followed she searched the chief's face for a reaction. It appeared he hadn't heard. After a moment or two he unlocked a bottom drawer and placed a file on the desk, "As you know, it's the practice of this delegation never to submit an adverse report unknown to the staff member. I was saving this until a date closer to your departure but as you have yourself raised the subject I'm obliged to read the pertinent items out. They are," he fingered the form, "Section A, Performance: One, Typographical errors, often as many as two in one sentence. Two, Lateness: Returned from lunch break at 3.05. Section B, Deportment: Spends excessive time away from desk. And now," he paused, "I must add a new Section C: Errors of Consequence. The word 'collateral' was transcribed as 'cultural loan' and," his voice rose in key, "When asked if this was her doing she informed us it was not and in so doing implicated an innocent party.'"

"I was troubled the day I typed those pages."

"'This gave,'" he went on, "'a misleading impression which not only halted negotiations but may have played into unforeseen developments.'"

Beula's presence of mind faded, making her voice shake, "What—which developments?"

"Body parts were found on the paramo. I don't propose to allow you details because it's restricted to Grades 7 and above." He smoothed down the file and reached for a paper clip," and nodding in dismissal picked up his pen.

Automatically she rose and crept to the door. Hand on doorknob, she turned slowly round, "There's…there's. There's something I want to say."

The chief made a fanning gesture to indicate brevity.

"With…regard to…unfore…fore-foreseen d-d-developments, if I'm not allowed details of the route your enquries took how can I know how much this err..err..error was due to me and..and…not due to m-me."

"I can't follow what you're saying."

"Well, my-my mis…mis…mis…mistakes are visible to them, so why didn't they didn't they see?"

"They? They see what?"

"Well, the…the c-c-cultural loan."

"The cultural loan was found. Why do you think we're having this conversation?"

"I mean, why not…earlier?"

He took up his pen, "I'm not here to answer moonstruck questions."

"But if my grade denies me access to—to—ah—reference points, how…"

Making large blinks Grapnel folded his hands under his chin.

"I mean, officers don't seem to be subject to the same…rules. My-my mistakes are visible to them but theirs aren't visible to m-me."

"There are no errors at executive level. That's why they're not visible."

Beula, breathing hard, looked at her feet, "Their work standards have no-no um-no-margin of error?"

"I'm talking about perfection," The chief's eyes shone, "I wonder if it's ever occurred to you that your salary and conditions may be far in excess of your capabilities?"

"But if officers paid twenty times my salary had done their job to perfection they would have found the typo." She found herself breathing easier, "And perhaps there wouldn't have been any need to bring in somebody like Dr. Medianoche."

The STD's pen remained suspended.

"I-I expect Personnel can clarify for me and explain my rights."

"Rights! You're answerable to this section to get the job done. As you haven't done the job to my satisfaction, as head of section, I have no option but to make another note under Section A Performance."

Beula raised her tone, "Is it p-perfection to offer me a lift home and when I hang back to…insist?"

"What has offering a junior employee a lift to do with the perfection of a job well done?" The chief looked tightly coiled yet entertained.

"To use my person as 'camouflage' was the word, I believe."

The Senior Trade Delegate steadied himself, "Under Section E, I may recommend Dismissal for Gross Insubordination. You'd lose by it, my girl. Pension rights for one·thing."

She advanced and leaned over his desk. Unblinking he met her stare and in the confrontation she saw another identity emerge much as she had seen around the mad parson. Embedded in the number one was the subaltern intimidated to the point where he'd turned into a bully.

"You've demonstrated incivility, dishonesty and incompetence," stated the young artilleryman.

Beula smarmed her hair down, "Uncivil because I'm not being treated civilly.

Yes, dishonest in not owning up but I'm owning up now and that makes me honest. As to incompetence, my mistakes must be teeny compared to those who would be perfect. No, Mr. Grapnel, I WILL have my say. LITTLE ONE, civility. Is it civil to have the Ladies room searched as if we have no right to privacy?" She started to pace, "Little two: Competence Is it competent to fail to find a typo on several drafts? Little three: Honesty. Are you being honest when, in the guise of a lift home you use me as a life preserver, with, unknown to me, a weapons bag next to my feet? As to terminating me don't you bother. I no longer have to type for a living. Because I'm Tendering My Resignation. On MARRIAGE." She scraped up her personnel file and sent it spinning across the desk.

36

The interview with Beula had left the Senior Trade Delegate in a state of shock, mottles barely visible. Chills scoured both sides of his face. He sat drumming for a while then rummaged for the humidor, changed his mind and pressed a button, "Ah, Phuff, I've just been informed of the Kettlehole engagement. Who is the party concerned? Is it the American she was with down at Fedoro's?"

The line was silent until Phuff's voice came on with gravity, "No sir. Never was a starter."

"It couldn't be Jooning could it? He and she were seen last Sunday evening coming out of the Ah Chum Chinese restaurant."

There was another pause until Phuff sighed, "I couldn't say, sir."

"You'd rule him out then?"

"Again sir, I can't say."

Grapnel sat a long time turning the spectacle of Jooning and Beula over in his mind before lifting the red exterior telephone.

"Get me Personnel London," he shouted at the switchboard, "Drop everything else. Hello there Gil. I'm calling with congratulations on your promotion. Personnel made a fine selection....Jeremy? A bit peaky...The separation's left him...well, how's Rowena standing up?...Ah, staying with you? Well, that's nice. I was never that close to my sister...Neither are you? Hahahaha. Well, that's what I called about. A posting might smooth things over...Has Rowena a preference?...Somewhere in Europe with a decent allowance, ah. Jeremy's choice was Abidjan or Quito...Oh, performance creditable. Saw Operation Hilda through with a certain amount of panache...Where did you say? Milan? Yes I read Ziggy Sweetland was kicked upstairs to New York, poor bugger. What influence do I have in Milan? You have the influence now, Gil. Though in point of fact I do know the Milan number one. Would I put in a word for Jeremy? Why would I not?...I'll be thanking you very much, Gil It's awfully good of you."

*

"Sit down, Jooning," Grapnel allowed him a cowrie shell smile. Jeremy grinned, trying to appear unconcerned. His heart leapt as the chief said with a careless air, "I suppose the good news must have come as a relief."

"News, sir?"

"Operation Hilda. Practically all the stuff showing up at respective fincas."

"Oh indeed I am relieved."

"I'm tending to agree," the chief went on, "that Don Fedoro's behavior has all along been...bizarre. Not turning over the original import license! As you may know, Uncle Pepe took him to task and the latest is he and Amo are in Miami to close a building purchase. In view of this I'm cancelling the notation on your personnel report." Grapnel put both hands (scabrous) on the desktop. (Stories via the worldwide grapevine held that he resulted from a failed abortion.) "I realize the incarceration must be pressing on your mind," Grapnel added, "On top of your wife's departure. With all that, we think you should be helped up the pole."

Jeremy paid full attention as the chief rattled a box of matches and balanced a half-smoked cigar, "We thought of scratching London. What they had in mind wouldn't have suited you. You'd have been no more than a glorified archivist. You didn't seem overthrilled about the posting, did you? What I thought is as follows," Jeremy's heart slowed as he watched Grapnel watching him, "There's a vacancy coming up in Milan. A plum post as you may know. Mind you, you'd have to put in a decent day's work but it's a transfer on promotion to head of section. You did your best for Operation Hilda and, in the event, things worked out. One thing I've observed. You go about things in a non-standard way. If they go crookedly amiss you stay with the original plan and somehow they revive. Unusual but..."

Alf Hapkin's off-key baritone rose above the chief's briefing:
"*Give me your Charlie Ryall,*
The lovelight in your mince pies,
Life never held
A fairer paradise."

Jeremy felt growing discomfort from a contradiction he could not pin down, conscience, on the side of uphill struggle involving deprivation, trying to convince him of his duty to return to London and the humdrum life, "...and I've been giving some thought to briefings with Ziggy in New York." Grapnel was saying, "Businesswise, Milan's dynamite. People go out at night. Dress up. Spend money. There's Ziggy's flat, a lovely ten-room penthouse on the Milanese scale, drawing room holds a hundred guests, married couple in help. I stayed with Zig last autumn." He rested his eyes on Jeremy for several seconds, then rose and patted him on the shoulder.

"You'll have the Scala. Years ago I was accredited there as a young sales clerk. My God how elegant were the women. From June the first they all went into sleeveless dresses cut to their curves. I used to linger in the Galleria with the idea of accosting one. I'd sit hours over a cognac. Old Pomeriggio, the number one, is only a twelve-month off retirement."

37

"I tell you, Beuly, I'm desperate. Desperate to get down to sea-level, can't wait to shed the not-quite-rightness I'm suffering, as though I've gone down to four cylinders. Touch wood, my stomach's quiet today and at times I feel more or less out of purgatory, thanks to you." Jeremy, lying full length on the floor of his music room, put out a hand.

After a while Beula got to her feet, "About our departure, I don't think we can put our talk off much longer," She switched on the table lamp.

Jeremy raised himself on one elbow, "What I had thought, darling, is as follows. My tour here ends officially end of November. However, I won't be arriving in London until the 7th of December because of briefings in New York.

"New York? It's the first I've heard of it."

"Dearest, I've only just found out. It's the last place on earth for me. All chiefs and no pals. You'd hate it. A do-it-yourself life at high speed. Anyway I can't be specific at this stage which means I can't tell you any more."

"Davison did say he'd be glad to make himself available as soon as we have a date."

"Davison?"

"The mad parson."

"We must beware of tempting the Fates."

Beula leant against the piano stool, "Will we move straight into the Maida Vale flat?"

"No darling, it's let until next September."

"I'm asking because I wondered if perhaps Nolita..."

"You're surely not thinking of taking a servant with you?"

"No. It's...I want to make things up to her. She's never in her life had anything new not even underwear."

"One thing at a time, Beuly. When does your tour end?"

"Officially 15th of May."

"You might find it more convenient to stay on and complete your tour."

Beula shook her head, "I absolutely can't."

Jeremy, turning over, examined the fleur de lys of the carpet, tracing patterns with a fingernail.

"I've given a month's notice," she added.

He looked round sharply, "A month's notice! Who to?"

"I told Hot Flash this afternoon."

"You can't go and resign just like that. You can't do that."

"Well, but it's done now."

"But why for God's sake? I mean, doesn't it occur to you that it might be ill-advised?"

"I told Grapnel the Cultural Loan was my idea, not Elna's."

Jeremy sighed, "It's what I feared."

"Now I'm supposed to believe it's all my fault that poor Don Renardo turns up in a parked vehicle on Calle 72."

"What I don't understand is why you didn't come clean in the first place. What could you have said?"

Beula shrugged, "I let him know that if bosses paid twenty times my salary did what they were paid to do they would have seen the typo first time round and that drug dealer would never have shown his face."

Jeremy came up to a sitting position.

"Furthermore, I told him I knew he used my person as a security shield."

A paler Jeremy sank back on the Chinese carpet, put hands under his head and rolled it back and forth, muttering under his breath, Why would I let you into it, if all you do is land me in the shit? Aloud he said, "It seems to me that you ought to cultivate what regard Grapnel has for you instead of endangering it. My impression is that as far as you're concerned, he's pliable."

"He's endorsed Dismissal on my personnel report," She sat in the lotus position between the piano stool and Jeremy.

He massaged his knees, "Darling, can't you play your cards any better than this?"

"I can't any longer go through life being careful."

"Because if you want to get reinstated you're going to have to apologize and ask him nicely to let you to stay on until the 15th of May."

"No more kowtowing to the gray suit, oh no. In any case he knows I'm resigning on marriage."

"On marriage?" Jeremy turned his body round, "To me?"

"I didn't specify." She propped herself against him, "Cross my heart your name never came up."

He lay staring at the frieze behind the piano. "Darling," he said, closing his eyes, "I wonder if you wouldn't mind going to the medicine cabinet in the hall cloaks and fetching me six grains of aspirin."

*

The senorita's leaving me this," Nolita held up a sand-colored mini-raincoat cut in the military style with abbreviated epaulets and brass insignia.

"You can't get on the bus dressed in something like that," Remedios cried, "Besides it'll never fit you."

Nolita held the raincoat tight to her chest swaying this way and that.

"Let me buy it from you."

"Buy it? You! With what?"

"Why would she want to get rid of it anyway? It's hardly been worn."

"Maybe she's getting promotion."

"To what? To Senora Green Eyes?"

Nolita folded her arms, a sign she was prepared to go no further.

PART TWO

38

New York City

Towards the end of December, having been in London six weeks, Beula at Heathrow Airport, was on her way to New York to meet Jeremy. Surrounded by travellers with trolleys piled high, and pushing out nagging doubts about aircraft staying up, she half-welcomed, half dreaded the call to board.

Despite Jeremy's non-arrival on 7th December, explained by a thirty-five minute telephone call, things had not, on the whole, gone too badly in the UK. Beula had acquired a somewhat reduced designer coat, shade of french mustard with matching crownless hat. Her mother's reaction to the engagement had been hard to read, despite Mrs. Kettlehole's avowal that it was her dearest wish.

Disdaining the cafeteria display of cakes and pastries, Beula took her herbal tea to a standing island, there to reflect not on another new post but a new life. Only let her get there, step into that world where one's

179

value lies in one's prospects. She brought out Jeremy's letter, creased and faded from much handling, telling of the offer of a delegation sublet in mid-Manhattan. She wasn't to worry about the felines even if Steno had tried to dive off the kitchen balcony on the day of departure. Nolita had handed the cats over to Juan Minuto believing their destination to be London. In person Jeremy had gone to the airport to transfer them. Both Steno and Yuri were settling in, looking forward to her homecoming.

Her friend Griz she had kept in the dark. Would cutting oneself off from employment appear to Griz any better than marrying on the rebound, blowing a money gift on a new motor car, getting a bridging loan? She was reluctant to let Griz into the correspondence with Personnel, the intimation that due to poor quality work and insubordination Beula had been terminated without pension rights, ending kindly with the phrase, 'I am so very sorry.'

Yesterday is history. Her new Italian shoes tip-tapped along interminable vinyl passageways, up slopes and down ramps, along a carpeted trailer into the belly of the great pulsating machine and the conditioned atmosphere of limitless service. But the plane seemed full of children, a toddler trying to take apart a pair of headphones, a tot tearing down the aisle distributing bubbly gum, the stewardess filling a bottle. Beula hesitated, "I wonder if I might move."

"One second, madam, I'll see."

Madam. It set the seal on her vision. Penthouse. Country club. Housekeeper. Eventually an aisle seat showed up at the back next to the toilets, beside an elderly couple in crumpled suits. The man had failed to remove his oversized stetson. She twisted her face into a resourceful grin.

*

Beula couldn't spot Jeremy at Arrivals. She was certain he was there in his invisible mode, deciding on the right moment to stand out. She trundled her cart to the edge of the barrier. Jeremy shouldn't be that hard to see. No man in the motley looked anything like him. Faces were

different. Wild-eyed, plasticky. The wait stretched to infinity The ele-
gance of her new outfit might make her appear an abandoned celebrity.
She put a hand to her throat. The plane had landed dead on time.

She'd wait in the Arrivals Lounge. But there was no Arrivals Lounge.
Or seating of any kind. Looking for a porter and seeing none, she gathered her bags and struggled up a winding staircase, one step at a time to
collapse in the first bucket seat on the balcony. She located herself at
Kennedy Airport, New York, felt the airport floor under her feet, the
stained red cushion under her rear, then got up and at the first cafeteria
counter called out, "Excuse me. I wonder if y-you would be g-good
enough to direct me to-to-to Enquiries." The waitress without looking
up continued to scrape pizza and ketchup from plates and crumple up
paper serviettes, "You talkin' to me? OK, you go downa staircase and
take a right."

Beula lugged the bags one by one to the ground floor. By now Jeremy
will have arrived and be looking for her. At an Information booth she
addressed the clerk: "Excuse me, but I wonder, c-could someone perhaps tell me if-if-if there's been a message for Beula Kettlehole?"

The large woman looked kind, "See that swing door over there? Go
through it, take a right and then a left. There'll be a Men's Room facing
you. Take another left and you'll see the message board."

The message board was a cylinder fluffed out with dog-eared notes
and cards. Beula put down her load and methodically read every
message in the K section, spending ten minutes decyphering various
handwritings. Shouldering one bag she pushed the other ahead with
her foot. The large lady was still in the Information booth.

"Excuse me..." Beula started to tremble, "There's no...no message
for me. Nothing's dated. Some of it I can't-can't make out."

"Duane," the lady called through a bullhorn, "C'mover here, will ya,
to booth four? Stay here Miss, I'll be right wich you." The booth was
cramped. She had trouble getting out when Duane arrived to take over.

"Now honey, don't cry," she handed Beula a paper towel, "Hey Enrico! Take this baggage to the lockers and give me the stub, d'ya hear?

"Now Miss, what ya must understand about the notice board is it changes every day so we don't need to date each message. Calls pour in all the time. What did you say your name was? Kettlehole, OK. What do we have here? Kellner, Kraus, Kemp, Krasdale, Kilbert, Kaye, we'll put that to one side. Kellogg. Kitchener. Now," she read out, "'Mrs. Kaye. In Washington. Please go to 792 West End Avenue, Apt 2X. I cannot meet you Larry.' Could that be yours?" Beula shook her head. The lady took out a bunch of keys and unlocked a door, approached a glassed-in area, calling out, "Foley. Tell Foley I want him."

A head bobbed up.

"Look up message 72."

She waited non-intrusively while the clerk thumbed through the tally, "Read it to me."

"Mrs. Kaye..."

"Give me the name of the caller."

"Looks like the name could have been Laramie."

She turned to Beula, "Laramie make sense to you?"

"I think so," Beula took out a peach-colored handkerchief and blew her nose.

The woman squeezed her arm. "Now away you go. Change your money over there. Here's the stub for the luggage. Don't lose it hon."

Beula took a minute to check on her reflection. Then after buying dollars, she stacked the bags in front of the automatic doors and struggled into the chilling air.

39

$\mathcal{N}$ight had fallen before the yellow taxi, speeding between the evenly-spaced green traffic lights, pulled up with a jolt beside a line of parked vehicles. Beula, peering at each bill, put the five dollars sixty in a slot attached to the driver's cage. It seemed quite a sum to pay for a ride from the bus terminal. The squat, swarthy doorman in a peaked cap standing inside the glass door watched her heave the suitcase. The taxi driver got out and dumped her holdall and paper carrier on the sidewalk. The doorman said with a sullen air, "Kettlehole you say? I got an envelope someplace. Here," He handed her a small bulky packet. Inside were three keys wrapped in a blank inter-office memo.

"Could you tell me where the lift is,?" she called in delicate tones.

"You're standing in front of it," he replied, not responding to her coquetry.

She ran this way and that, moving her bags into the elevator. She heard mewing the minute she got out. As she wrestled with the first key, the desire to get inside brimmed over. Once she'd overcome the yale lock, there was the mortise until at last the sticky little door jumped open and the two black cats flew into the passage, the larger one walking over her suitcase, the leaner one trying to get into the paper carrier. Travel-exhilarated, Beula ran in, parked her bags and sat down with the cats to see how they looked. A little on the thin side and desperately pleased, one rubbing its head on her sleeve, the other licking her hand.

Several things struck Beula about the apartment. It was stifling. All lights were on. The proportions seemed pretentious: high skirting boards, even a length of wainscoting whose motif had all but been obscured by fifty coats of paint. Two doors in the anemic hall, one of which was a cupboard; the other, tall and skinny, its glass transom painted over, led into an undersized living room with a lofty ceiling. The place was a fragment sliced from a stately room. Lifting the blind, she looked out at a forlorn, truncated Christmas tree down on the sidewalk. A tall, thin radiator fizzed away in a corner. There was a smell of old cooking. She took a dining chair, balanced herself on the window ledge and tried to pull down the top window which was painted shut. She stared at her watch a long time.

Removing her mustard Harrods coat, she opened the hall closet. Inside hung one of Jeremy's suits, the tan gabardine. She took it out and held it close, breathing it in, dancing around with it. What should she make for their supper? All she could find in the kitchen cubicle, besides catfood, was an unopened packet of grape nuts, ditto of petit beurre biscuits, and a canister of Earl Grey Tea. In the refrigerator three bottles of *Entre Deux Mers*. She sank onto the spongy bed, pulled off her boots and lay on the covers. The cats interrupted their grooming to walk on her and around her, finally settling down.

A small chip of plaster fell from the ceiling onto her pillow. Five minutes to three in the morning. He'd tried and failed to get in because she'd mistakenly set the catch on the front door. He'll come back after eight in the morning.

The cupboard under the sink yielded up a stained saucepan. Beula scoured it carefully and lit the single-ring gas cooker. Whoever cleaned the apartment hadn't cared any more than the person who'd painted the woodwork. No tackling of grime between cracks. She sorted her items into categories: underwear including nightgown; scarf, gloves and sewing case. Opening the top drawer of a dresser she found a pair of cockroaches clambering over Jeremy's hairbrush. Her heart turned over and she ran back to the living room. By ten o'clock in the morning he still hadn't rung. Little chores like ironing her winter slacks had helped to stave off anxiety. She turned to the kitchenette. Hardly had she started scrubbing around the gas jets when there came a firm ring at the door.

"Thank God," she cried, rinsing her hands under the hot tap, drying them on her handkerchief, running to unbolt the door. Outside stood a youngish unisex person holding a stepladder. Small with dark frizzy hair, dot eyes and a long jaw like a horse.

"Do you need rooms painted? Special new biodegradable water-based?"

"Rooms painted!" Beula couldn't contain her emotion, "No, I don't want rooms painted," she shouted, "It's the last thing in the world that I want." She slammed the door, rebolted it, and ran weeping to the bedroom.

Sometime after twelve noon the doorbell rang again. Beula patted her face with a tea towel. Too exhausted to repair with lipstick and comb she scraped her hair back and, holding herself steady, unbolted the door, opening it wide.

It was the same unisex individual with the crinkly hairdo and little round eyes.

"I heard you crying. No, don't close the door. I live in the building. I'm in 2W. Listen I've been through it all. When I came to the city, I cried for days at a time. I only came from Queens but I know what you're going through. I'd invite y'over for cawfee but jeez my place is really really disorderly."

Beula blew her nose as she looked about for a teapot.

"Don't worry about that. 'Erb tea, Sanka, whatever ya got. Water's OK if you have a filter. I'm Emery, by the way, originally Anne-Marie. I'm English myself. Pleased to meet you. Mom and I came over when I was two. I remember things like trolley buses and bubble and squeak. But if I get too specific it dates me." She took two steps to the center of the living room and looked around, "You've got a kitty. Wow! You can smell my Tyrone can't you?"

"I found this," Beula held up a large terracotta teapot made in Japan, "I'm heating some water and fortunately there are some semi-sweet biscuits."

Emery strutted round the living room, hands in pockets, collar turned up though the thermostat was stuck at seventy-two. She had, Beula noticed, beautiful hands. "Well, don't I know men are real trouble," she was saying to the cat, "Sometimes I try to figure out what's right with them." she inspected Jeremy's suit hanging on a coat hook. "Wow, Savile Row? The guy must be some kind of swell!"

"Are men here less trouble than in Britain," Beula wondered.

Emery thought for a bit, "My dad was big trouble according to Mom. Used to say things like, What makes you think you can draw, write poetry, whatever? Whereas my kid might say, 'Don't exhibit yet,' or 'Do we need two T.S. Eliots in the house?'"

"Will you have tea after all? It is made."

"Seems to contract my bladder. All right then I'll take the first cup."

Beula had set out an elaborate table, cucumber sandwiches, tinned Christmas cake found at the back of the refrigerator, had poured bottled water for the teapot and laid out Jeremy's two Royal Doulton cups. She sat across from Emery, checking from the minute hand that the allotted brewing time did not overrun. Presently she lifted the teapot, changed her mind and took the milk jug. The liquid in the translucent cup glowed palest sepia, then golden brown. Not only was it at the correct temperature, that is a touch below scalding, but the brew was perfect. Two swallows and all's right with the world. Jeremy's arrival was imminent. Not only did his closet verify, there were his two locked briefcases. She breathed a sigh of anticipation and Steno, sensing her mood, stole across the back of the easy chair and in slow motion crept under her arm. Beula sat upright, suspended in her culture and her time, cheeks flushed, eyes inert in front of the individual sprawled on the loveseat. "...kneading me around hoping to find a lump...took out this long item like a dog's nose...didn't get my consent to a pap smear. Anytime I need ante natal he's there..."

At Beula's moment of caffeine-induced well-being, the telephone began to clamor. She drained the cup and poured out another before rising. Lifting the receiver she kept in mind Jeremy's caution about revealing identity.

"Ze senor is not here," she said, "You are his lawyer? Well then, I take ze number. You are from where? Tetuan? Oh Jeremy, can this really be you? Yes, I suppose I am...coping, well, surviving. Just."

She ran to the loveseat and embraced her new-found friend. Emery patted her lightly, "There, there. I know, I know. Well, I guess I gotta get back to business. I got to finish a floor-through. The bedroom I haven't even started. I get the job Friday. They want it finished Saturday night. How do you like the time frame? The roller I can deal with but the cutting in? I could lose my cool."

*

As she prepared for Jeremy's arrival, Beula's happiness permeated the neighborhood. Broadway became a mecca for ethnic take-out food, Riverside Park planted with beautiful twisted trees, West End Avenue dignified, the apartment a haven of warmth and convenience, the streets full of characters from Warner Brothers Films. It had taken a whole day to clean the microkitchen. The stovetop alone took three hours. As she scrubbed and scrubbed with fierce joy, visions of life in Milan began to take shape. Getting into the swim might not be straightforward, particularly if any delegation wife had known Rowena. She did not know how soon after the divorce she would arrive. What she did know was there'd be no more scouring and scrubbing. She could not believe Jeremy was actually going to be in the apartment. Standing on this very spot, smelling of exclusive clubs, grand hotels. Barely had she completed her toilet when the intercom gave a piercing blast, not unlike the STD's buzzer. She pressed the button once and held her breath. A voice, brash and nasal, shouted, "Bring money to pay the cab."

"Who's speaking?"

"Henry the doorman. Your friend's arrived." The machine clicked off.

A taxicab was idling behind a medium truck. She could see Jeremy hunched in back. When he spotted her, he leaned forward to open the door. The air was Arctic and she couldn't feel it. Between a black astrakhan helmet pulled down and a muffler, only his nose protruded. He felt like a dead weight. In the elevator she pulled up his helmet and they embraced. There were gray crevices around his eyes.

"I'll run you a hot bath," she murmured as they rolled foreheads.

"That would be heavenly, darling. And perhaps find me a wee dram of something that I might live? I believe there's a bottle in the bedside cabinet right at the back. Another thing, my head feels feverish. Did you pack a thermometer?" Leaning on her, he led to the bedroom where he lay down carefully.

"There's something I've realized," he told her after he had drunk the brandy, "If I try to expand into higher purposes, the tendency is to attract various illnesses. I mean, this cold's waiting to turn into flu. If it is flu, it could develop into pneumonia." He took her hand, "I'd got us tickets to Figaro," He began singing in a cracked falsetto, "*No so piu cosa son cosa faccio.*"

"Oh Jeremy, we can't possibly go out."

He sank gratefully down among the pillows, while she unwound his muffler, undid overcoat and jacket. He propped his feet up for her to pull off his boots.

"Take the trousers too. Otherwise they'll get creased. Here's my tie. It lives in the wardrobe." With an effort he sat up as she helped him off with shirt and undershirt, very slowly got to his feet and stumbled to the bathroom. Even in his enfeebled state there was confusion all around. His clothes and objects seemed to fill the apartment.

"Did you warm the bathtowel on the radiator? You did? Good. Fetch me another wee droppie, will you?" He tested the bathwater, stepped in, and lay down in the tub like a dead man. Soon he opened his eyes and put out a hand. His body looked more tanned than she remembered. "Come, sweetheart, and perch somewhere. Get yourself a glass of vino. There's a bottle of white in the fridge."

Beula hurried out and returned with a kitchen stool which she unfolded and placed next to the bathtub then went in search of the wine.

He raised his glass, "Thank heavens we don't have to worry about drafts and things. Remember those bathrooms at school that used to fill with steam?"

She clicked his tumbler, "I'm drinking to our life together."

"To our life together," he echoed, draining the brandy glass.

"Any news from south of the border?"

"News?" he frowned.

"What about Camber?"

"What about him?"

"Is he well?"

"I suppose so."

"Did his wife come back?"

"Eventually yes. Something of a beauty." Jeremy leant forward to turn on the hot water tap, "Sort of swarthy. Not my type." He stretched up and took the drink, "Elna got promotion to Secretary 2."

Beula stared at her foot against the wall, "Any news of Nolita?"

"Nolita. Ah yes. Found a job with the Brazilian consulate and although she isn't overimpressed with the scene, they have gadgets."

"A vacuum cleaner."

"Yes and something else. A carpet washer."

"Jeremy, can you imagine what I've been through. It's so confusing here. Like the Third World without help."

"Didn't I say that very thing? Well darling, I chose this section because Trade Office people don't usually venture this far uptown, so if we dine out here, there's a slim chance of my being seen and even if I were, of being recognized." He felt around in the bathwater for the soap, "Beuly, I'm afraid I'll have to go straight to bed."

She passed him the heated towel. "Can I fetch anything from the late-night chemists?"

"Don't think so. I've had a dose of Influgonex and it's making me sleepy. I can't face food. But I would like a spot more wine, a decent drop."

"But if you're taking antibiotics you shouldn't have brandy or wine. I'd better make you a hot drink."

She turned out the light and stole back to the living room, found the sugar and a lemon, took out a tin of catfood and, struggling with the can opener, felt she wouldn't be anywhere else in the world. After cleaning the bath, she heated some pearl barley, opened a packet of Birds Eye peas and, seeing Jeremy bedded down for the night, unfurled the sofabed, found a single sheet and thanking Providence for good fortune, made up her bed.

At two in the morning she felt Jeremy bending over her. Rapturously she held him as he murmured against her hair that he felt locked in the dungeon at Hangar Six.

"Get in with me."

"Darling, I can't. Got to get to a hospital."

"What?"

"You must get me to the nearest casualty department."

"I don't know any casualty department."

"Look it up in the phone book."

She found the light switch, looked about for his jacket and overcoat but could not find them, the telephone book, her stockings, or his helmet.

Twenty minutes later they reached the lobby. After a long wait on the corner she managed to flag down a cab and help Jeremy, wrapped in a blanket, to hobble into the polar night.

"Where did you say you wuz goin'?"

"To the nearest hospital," Beula said firmly.

"Which one is that?"

"I don't know. I wonder if you know."

"I'm gonna ask my radio service."

The cab had the feeling of a prison cell but warm. Beula huddling close to Jeremy, wrapped the blanket tighter to stop the shuddering, "What are your symptoms? she whispered.

"I only hope I don't freeze to death. Yet I'm sweaty and, oh darling, I'm at the bottom of a well."

The voice on the squawkbox told them to go to the nearby Memorial Hospital. The cab circled a driveway and slid down a ramp to a tunnel marked Emergency. In the brightly-lit waiting room they sat and sat, Jeremy growing grayer, falling asleep waking with a jolt and moaning. The other outpatients were of a kind she'd never seen, worse off than Alf Hapkin, wretched, bloated, faceless. At about three thirty, a slight, twisted man fell out of the revolving door and patted his way along the line of seats to the counter, "I need help now. NOW," he called in a thin, reedy voice. The night clerk said in an inflexible way that he must take his turn along with the rest. The man sank onto the nearest chair. His head dipped forward and stayed like that a long time. Eventually a white-coated medic bent down and held his wrist, "Dead," he pronounced, "Did he get a number?"

"Yeah, I gave him thirty three. You better have them take him out."

"Oh God," Beula said out loud. She walked over to the desk, changed her mind and sat down again, "Perhaps I should look for another hospital," she said to the warhorse next to them.

"I wouldn't do dat," the woman told her, "You seen one, you seen all," She jerked a thumb, "What's with the guy?"

"My feet are cold," Jeremy muttered. When Beula bent down to lace up his shoes he asked to be taken to the Men's Room. As she helped him to his feet and escorted him to one of the stalls, his knees sagged and urine leached through his pyjamas to the tile floor. She opened his pyjama trousers, shouting "There's no towel in here." Without removing them, she wrung out his trousers and wiped him and the floor with the paper serviette she'd salvaged from the airline meal.

At five minutes to seven the night clerk shouted Jeremy's number. They shuffled into a cubicle where a young man in green overalls helped hoist Jeremy onto the aluminium table. After an examination the doctor put his stethoscope side, "He seems to have an allergic reaction to medication. I recommend he force liquids—a mixture of lemon and cranberry juice mixed with bottled water. That'll be ninety-four dollars."

"Ninety four dollars!"

"A check will do as long as we have telephone number and ID. Driver's license will do."

Hands trembling she went through Jeremy's coat pocket, pulling dollar bills from his wallet.

*

Towards the end of the afternoon, the patient having consumed nine pints of liquid, lay smiling from the pillows, "I won't be strong enough to go out to dinner but at least I should eat something. Is there anything?"

"Bread, cheese and salad. I could get knishes."

"Could you make me the welsh rarebit you told me about, the sort you put beer in? Which reminds me, I could just about sink an imported lager."

By six o'clock he was sitting up, "I'd better be damn careful I don't take that drug again. It bloody near saw me off. I would have had to cancel my briefings."

"Briefings?"

"Well, Washington and Milan."

"But you…"

"Let me explain. After my five-day conference in Washington, I'm supposed to be going to Milan tonight to report, returning at the week-end."

"You can't possibly go. You'll never be able to concentrate."

"Darling, don't say 'never.' Especially not here."

"What's going to happen to me?"

"We'll be here another six weeks."

"But how can you think of leaving me alone?"

"Well, the celebrities seem to like it. To some it's a relief to be faceless."

"Not to me, Jeremy."

Hands clasped behind his head, he chuckled as Yuri walked across his chest.

"How long before we leave?" she cried.

"The divorce is coming along."

"I'll scream if you say that again."

"Sweetheart, the rent's paid until the end of Jan. Are you all right for money?"

"Down to sixty seven dollars."

"That should see you through for a week or two."

"You must mean see *us* through."

"And if push comes to shove you could always get temp work."

"Temp work? I come all this way to join you only to be told to get temp work! My God, I pay my own airfare. I buy food for two out of my own money."

"Darling bear in mind the whole situation is Temporary. Listen if the welsh rarebit's too difficult, make me a toasted cheese sandwich and I'll see if I can stand. See if I can still get on the night flight. It might not be that draining. I'd get there for the afternoon meeting, having embraced Morpheus on the jet."

"But," she cried, You can't leave me here like this. You can't. I've only just arrived."

"Darling, so have I, in a manner of speaking."

"I believe it's New Year's Eve."
"So it is, sweetheart. Happy New Year."

"Emery," Beula called out, as she ran to release the catch on the door, "I'm here. How are things?"

"How do I know? You got juice?"

"Lemon barley water."

"Did you say you had a water washer?"

Beula shook her head. Handing Emery a mixture of barley water and tonic she tried to attend to an account of Claudine, the big client owning fourteen apartment houses who wants a bathroom papered in patterned satin finish, seventy bucks the walls but because the paper wasn't prepasted it ought to have been eighty-five but it's no good needling the big client because she's got it in mind to turn over the choice of wallpapers to Emery. "Are you okay?" Emery added after a lull, "You don't look so hot."

Beula sighed, "New Year's Day was a trial. I keep trying to think up a suitable Resolution. Well Jeremy's returning Saturday morning and it's already Tuesday. We're supposed to be leaving in exactly five weeks." She paused for Emery to ask about their departure, then added, "We're off to Milan."

"Where?"

"Milan in the north of Italy."

"Ah, Mint Milano."

"But do you know while I was tidying up I discovered something odd. His tan gabardine suit and his two briefcases are nowhere in the apartment. I've looked everywhere."

"I guess the guy took them with him," Emery said through an unparalleled yawn.

"How could he if I packed his overnight bag? I distinctly remember putting in pyjamas, an extra jacket, the rest of a bottle of Remy Martin. Perhaps I ought to telephone Milan and ask him. Trouble is he didn't leave a number." She clapped her hands, "But his office'll have it." She lifted Yuri from the telephone book and began flicking through with her long, frosty nails, "Ah, MTO." She moved the cat from the open page and, with a pencil, dialled the number. While it was ringing she scratched at a mark on the tiny table. After twelve rings a hurried American voice answered.

"I'm calling because I need a number where a staff member can be reached. His name is Jeremy Jooning. I could leave word with his office and they could call the Milan office."

There was a click and a voice came on, "Jooning speaking."

*

Beula put the phone back with a clatter, "Emery, please." She flew down the corridor and banged on 2W. After a while the door inched open enough to hear Emery say, "I'm busy right now. Tyrone's decided to crouch."

"Emery I need help. Something's happened. It's…" her voice failed. Under the fluorescent, two new lines were imprinting Beula's face from nose to chin. Shadows deepened around her mouth.

"Give me five minutes, okay?" After a lot of rustling Emery backed out and locked the door, with "Now what is it?"

"I can't go on like this."

"Where's your apartment key? You left the door open? You must never do that, you hear? I can't help you if you make all that noise. We gotta stay calm. Let's go back to your apartment. Ah, on the latch! Sit here and let it all hang out. Let me do something for you. I know, I'll make you a nice cup of tea a la British. I know to warm the teapot. One teaspoon and one for the pot. In a couple minutes you'll be as right as ninepence. How's that for Oldy English? Now you have a good cry. There's nothing like it for beauty. As long as you don't scream. That hanky's undersized. Don't you have tissues? Wait," She went out and returned with a dish towel.

In a choking voice Beula tried to speak.

Emery patted her, "I know. I know."

"It's…It's…" Content was lost in upwelling which rose to a crescendo, diminished then started up again. Only when she had accepted the china teacup and saucer, could she speak.

*

"I am not staggered," Emery said, "I am not totally dumbfounded. I've heard of every kind of chicanery. But I will say this. I am unfamiliar with anything like this guy's machinations. He comes in, takes his things and leaves? I mean how could you get mixed up in this? You so refoined."

"I'd hardly been out of the flat, Anne-Marie. Once to Zabars. And while I was out you think he might have slipped in and removed his stuff? No, he couldn't stoop that low."

"The shmuck's in New York incomunicado ain't he?"

Beula had another burst, gradually calming down as Emery poured out a second cup.

"My advice is as follows: Tune him out. It's not that onerous. Here's a New Year's Affirmation. Look at me. Say after me: *I Am Above This Kind of Shit.* My God, do you think I haven't been through this? One day my Manny comes home from the store and announces he's returning to California, just like that. I'm struck dumb but once it sinks in I ask does he mean a short visit? And you know what the asshall says? His mother sub-let her apartment on West 64th Street."

Beula patting her eyes, sat up and tried to pay attention.

"So he QUITS HIS JOB. Takes two days to pack up her stuff and hops on the first plane to Oakland just like that. I had to take myself by the throat, tell myself it's not worth my energy, not worth my time. **I Am Above This Kind of Shit.**"

*

After Emery left, Beula selected a grapegreen eyeliner and drew the tiny foam applicator across the rim of her eyelids, brushed creamy powder under her eyebrows, a dab on the chin, a speck of bronzetone pressed powder to the tip of her nose. With lips pearly, cheeks in madder crimson, chignon artfully extended to conceal unretouched roots, she drew on her new french mustard coat with its youthful collar and chic crownless hat. She'd called the MTO in advance, an innocuous telephone enquiry which drew a blank, then the invented muddle where she'd pretended to call from inside the delegation. From this she had learned that Jeremy worked there nine to five, that his office was on the 15th floor and he was now in it.

At four fifty she reached the lobby and stood well back from the 9-19 bank of elevators in order to see him before he saw her. He was scared to death. That was the key to his collapse. She'd guide him to that ground level restaurant with the funny name. She'd call forth the nature of the obstacles he imagined were in his way and they would talk it out if it took all night.

The elevators began disgorging personnel. Beula, pinned against the wall by the rush, searched the face of every dark-haired man of medium height. Five minutes later, fearing he had come down via another elevator she transferred to beside the revolving door but soon had to fight her way back to the original spot. By five twenty the cleaning crews were wheeling in equipment. Soon all elevators were still. A doorman took out a tall flick brush and pan. Her over-visibility made her want to creep away.

"You lookin' for somebody, lady?"

"Just a friend," she made her voice crisp.

"Which floor?"

"Fifteenth."

"Wyncher go up and talk to reception? Oh wait, no their elevator closes at five fifteen."

She had to feed the cats and buy something for her supper. But she didn't want any supper, neither could she face another evening in. Tears blurring her view, she almost walked into the revolving door. Outside, the stinging cold held back grief as she crept north on Park Avenue, unsure of how to find the apartment.

*

At four fifty the next afternoon she was back in the lobby in the same coat but wearing a black bandanna. This time she stayed in full view of elevators 9-19, checking heads with care. There were one or two Jeremy look-alikes with his unruly hair and bulging forehead. At five ten she stepped into the elevator and got out at the fifteenth floor. The reception clerk sat in a crepuscular hall lit like Aladdin's cave. Mr. Jooning had left, she was told. Took the elevator? Of course he took the elevator. How else would he get down to the car park?

On Thursday at five, Beula rode down to the basement level and posted herself at the glass partition facing the exit lane. It was a smallish garage, all four walls in focus. Autos were either brand new or highly polished. Sticking it out, despite life-threatening fumes, she finally caught sight of Jeremy approaching from another direction acccompanied by a spindly man with red hair. Heart racing, she stepped off the platform and ran towards them but they had already ducked into a low sports car. As it went into reverse she had to dodge behind a stanchion to avoid being knocked down.

*

"Hanging around in a parking garage," Emery exclaimed, "I don't believe this. After I give you advice. Advice worth a fee!"

"I'm on the high seas in a coracle," Beula murmured.

"If you can't live without confrontation, all you have to do is go to the guy's office and sit there till he comes out."

*

At one thirty on the Friday afternoon, Beula began to get pins and needles, having spent an hour or more thumbing through 'Racing Car,' 'Scientific American' and 'New York Magazine.' She rose and limped to the elevator."

"Will you be back?" the receptionist called from the cavernous public area.

Avoiding her eyes, Beula said in a faraway voice, "Not today." The elevator doors sprang open without a sound and the chamber zoomed down to the ground floor non-stop. While it waited she thought for a bit then pressed fifteen. As she approached the deserted reception desk, Jeremy's extension number came to her. Three-six. She pushed open the half door and made her way down the corridor past drinking fountain and Men's Room to a sign 1536-40. Without knocking, she pushed open door 36. Jeremy looked up from a desk hedged in by paper. In the moment after he'd locked the door, she was in his arms. They remained still a long time. He held her gently, whispering, "Oh darling darling, it's been such a long long work week." After the crescendo of emotion had tailed off, he drew her down on a small padded bench.

"I must look awful," she said at last.

"Darling you don't," He reached over to his desk, opened a drawer and took out a carved box made in Algeria, "I keep your letters in here. Whenever I feel low I can take them with me to lavatories, to places where they sing."

Seeing him bent over her last letter, she said, "I'm here to-to ask you s-something"

His color had improved and his smile showed new teeth, "Well let's have it."

"Well I…It's…Did you come to the flat recently…and take back your tan suit and the briefcases?"

"If you look around you'll see them there somewhere. Darling, stop looking so woebegone."

"I…I have to know if…if you came and r-removed the suit and the briefcases."

"Dearest I didn't."

"Where did you go when you left me on New Year's Eve?"

"I told you I had to go to Milan."

"Did you put it in your…calendar?"

"I don't work like that."

"What time did you…get there?"

"Milan? Somewhere in the early hours."

"I wonder if you really…really went."

"Did I get there? Yes I got there…but late. Luckily the meeting got postponed until three in the afternoon so I was able to get some shuteye."

"But didn't you say it was an…an afternoon meeting?"

"Lunchtime really. Scheduled for one, not three o'clock."

"I rang your office Tuesday morning and your voice answered."

"Darling, you're being fanciful."

"I'm telling you I heard your voice say 'Jeremy Jooning.'"

"That's Ziggy Sweetland, my oppo. Bit of a wag."

"Sounded like you," Beula patted under her eyes.

"Well the physical entity has been in Milan all week."

"On Monday they said you were in your office."

"That's the new receptionist for you."

"I saw you yesterday in the garage. A little after five."

"It's a bloody funny place to wait."

"Where are you staying?"

"In between whiles I doss down at the Sweetlands."

"Is he the one you're taking over from? Ziggy?"

"The same."

"Why don't you get briefed here?"

"That's what I'm doing."

"Did you visit South America before being posted there?" He walked to the window and stood with his back to her, "You're in New York for briefings so what's the point of going to Milan?" Her question reverberated and he put his hands over his ears, She started weeping again, "Why have you kept me in the dark?"

"Have you had lunch? Mmm? Look at me. Have you? No. Tell you what. Let's go out and get a bite. If you'd like to wait at reception I'll come…" he cut himself off, seeing her look. "All right, lovey, we're off. No, we can't go to the West Womb. Well, perhaps we can. It should be quiet by now, and if we're seen, you're…"

"A former colleague," she blew her nose.

*

It was almost three and the West Womb was down to a couple of waiters. Over two glasses of dark Mexican beer and a small Greek salad, her spirits had rallied to the point where she felt casual enough to drop a "When would I join you?"

He hardly paused as he said, "I can't come up with a date because I don't know myself, but with the uncertainty of things it might be at the drop of a hat."

"Any progress on the divorce?"

"Well that's just it. There's been one delay after another. Rowena never returns her solicitor's phone calls and mine says that unless she decides to change her plea, we may be in for a wait."

"I thought she left you."

"Yes but she didn't show up for the hearing."

"Can't we…just dispense with the divorce?"

"Beuly, I'll have to be getting back soon. I've got a pile of paper to read for a five o'clock meeting."

"Will I see you at the apartment?"

"Can't make it tonight, I'm afraid. There's the Sweetlands dinner party."

"Could you pop over afterwards?"

"It's a bit dicey."

"What about tomorrow."

"I'm not sure how many appointments I have."

"On a Saturday?"

Beula had got unusually flushed and her great eyes shone as she reached over to his side of the table, "You know the MTO wouldn't restore my pension rights don't you?"

"Well who authored that"

"The Delegation isn't a totalitarian state. I expected a few rights."

"Do you think I had a few rights when I found myself in that dungeon? I don't suppose it got through to you that it was Fedoro who did that to me all because of you?"

She smiled into her beer then, looking up, burst into little shrieks of laughter, stopping and starting, getting shrill.

"Don't get hysterical I beg of you. There may be people here from the office."

"I can't believe," she held her stomach, "the catastrophes originating with Beula Kettlehole." Breathing deep, she stretched her arms over her head and surveyed Jeremy's pointed eyebrows, green eyes half-closed, splayed nose, frizzy hair half hiding his ears. Leaning forward she parted the salt and the serviette dispenser, "Remember Beula the Muse, Beula the All-Knowing? What was she to you? Aside from glandular. Eh?"

He smiled into the painted beer glass.

Late-night music filtered in from somewhere. She sat clutching the salt and the metal dispenser, chin low to the table, "Getting back to Rowena."

Jeremy stared at the table, pallid, long-faced.

"Will Rowena's delays mean we may never...never get off the ground?"

He looked from side to side, finally saying, "No doubt it is a factor."

"A factor of what? That she's bringing things to a halt? Or we shall never get to Milan?"

"Well, both really."

Beula tossed the salt shaker and serviette dispenser over both shoulders, lifted her cup and emptied black coffee over Jooning's head. Then, sending a plate and glass flying, with both hands she gripped his shirt collar. He rose to restrain her, knocking the table over. She extricated her left hand and managed to punch him in the face. One near his nose for not meeting her at the airport; one just missing his eye for sneaking in and taking his things; one in the teeth for lying about Milan; one behind an ear for leading her on about the divorce.

The bartender froze behind the cocktail bar where the disturbance was amplified by shivering bottles and glasses. The maitre D and chef rushed out of the kitchen, one Hispanic, the other black, the former severe and disapproving, the latter keenly interested. A couple three tables away, after a lingering glance, continued their exchange.

Untangling himself from Beula, the panting Jeremy stood facing her. Then swallowing hard he shouted for the check, dragged out his wallet and pushed a hundred dollar bill onto the waiter, with handwaving to convey that no change was necessary. Beula's hair, graying at the roots, had sprung out in all directions, leaving a bronze-colored donut pinned in place. Eyeshadow had run below her lower lids. Streaks of coffee and splotches of cream clung to the front of her trouser suit. Deeply flushed, she threw the french mustard coat over her shoulders and flounced to the exit, stopped then returned for her purse.

Jooning, scratched and downcast, wiped coffee from under his collar and tie.

"I think I'm losing my mind," she panted.

"Luckily the place is nearly empty," he muttered, peering down the front of his shirt, scrubbing hair and neck with a paper mat.

"I can't live without seeing you twice a week," she screamed, "And it's my birthday in a fortnight's time."

"I'll be there for it." Fishing out two more hundred dollar bills, he stuffed them into her coat pocket then backed away excusing himself and muttering, "Anyone can see I do my best. Why do they have to put me to the test?" She watched until the Men's Room door swung to a close.

Outside, the air felt softer. She was able to walk across town without the cold tensing her shoulders. Emotionally discharged, she took long strides, holding her head up. There was cleaning to do, sorting out. She'd get frozen cannelloni for supper.

41

*I*t was Beula's second week in the temp slot. Through Emery's contact she'd been introduced to somebody called Hed who had a discretionary budget. The pay was $3.61 an hour but there was no tripping around with cups of coffee and she was to answer the telephone with her own name. Her life had taken on a temporary routine. Setting the alarm for six, she shampooed her hair, got to the desk twenty minutes before opening time, put herself and cats to bed at 9.30 except for the Mondays and Fridays that she and Jeremy met. After the scene in the West Womb Jeremy had seemed a lot more relaxed. Arrived on time, took her to ethnic eating places on the Upper West Side, expressed optimism about their future. Celebrated her birthday at a Latino restaurant.

On this Monday at noon, going in to water the poinsettias, she noticed a new name on Hed's door. He had been "let go." Had breezed in that morning at 8.40 and by 11.15 simply disappeared. The receptionist explained that as the company could no longer afford him, his job had been revamped for a qualified female consultant. The new boss turned out to be a nubile miss with waist-length hair calling herself Doctor.

Jeremy was to collect Beula that evening at the usual time, 6.30, but had not telephoned to confirm. She called his office twice and he had not returned the calls. She had waited in the apartment until 7.30 then ordered yellow rice and black beans from the Creole take-out. There was no return phone call on Tuesday. Or Wednesday. The mini-skirted doctor looked Beula over with a boss's eye and began summoning her in for dictation three or four times a day.

By Thursday a change had come over Beula. Withdrawn in the coffee line and the Ladies Room, she had cut out the hairwash. Rising at eight rather than at six she dropped eye shading and rouge from the routine, showing up at the office in the same getup. She no longer checked up on shoes, pantyhose or nail varnish. The stringy hair and seated clothes made a difference to the way the colleagues responded to her. Instead of, "Gee, that color looks great on you," or "I love yer voice," the receptionist came over to ask how she liked her coffee or tea.

With a paper cup of Earl Grey in front of her she placed a fifth call at Jeremy's office, learning for the fifth time he was away from his desk and telling the operator she had mislaid the Sweetlands' number and did they have it handy? Marshalling her nerve, she dialled the Sweetland home. "Jeremy's gone," said a hoarse voice, "Where? Transferred to Milan. He and Rowena left last Sunday. Would you like their number?"

42

All activity became remote as if the sound was turned down. Colleagues waded about in a mist. Somebody wanted out but conditioning warned, do nothing. Beula sat silent, screaming inside. The telephone rang and she grabbed it.

"Will you come in for some dictation?"

Automatically she took up her pen and notepad and, breathing hard, pushed open the door to Hed's former office. The doctor, looking about nineteen, in a tight-fitting silk suit, hair trailing over the telephone, changed her mind innumerable times, looking straight through Beula throughout. The combination of trailing hair and flawless legs crossed patriarchal style on the desk made Beula feel strange. The day before she'd put a bald head and moustache on the young boss. Her own head was scraping the ceiling. With the doctor murmuring into the telephone, Beula made herself blank out where she was by tuning out the conversation. But one sentence broke through, "Sure it's okay to tell me. There's nobody here. Except a secretary."

The secretary rose. The boss fixed her with a restraining eye and delaying arm to no avail. Throwing open the door, Beula strode down the corridor to her bay, pulled her coat from the line of pegs and strutted to the elevator.

*

At the 86th Street subway exit, she hesitated. Somewhere in the thorax faint palpitations gave notice of shortness of breath. Nodding her head every few seconds, she stood panting on the top step while passengers filed past on either side.

Suddenly she cried, "I Am Above This Kind of Shit." The breathing eased somewhat. She opened her Harrods coat and unbuttoned her sweater. The weather must be unseasonably warm. As she waited to cross Broadway, a hard hat sheltering in a doorway shot her a glance of stony appraisal. At the traffic island she stared at a small old man resting on a bench. "He never ever lived in that grimy little flat," Beula shouted. The elder on the bench went on chewing, "And I know what he hoped for. He hoped and prayed I'd never land." Without waiting for the WALK sign, with a tremulous laugh, she strode across Broadway making a blue bus, yellow taxi and plumber's van pull up in a hurry.

Wearing a reasoning expression, knotting her face, pumping her jaw, she lowered her tone, "Do I look like Ms. Nobody? I do, don't I?" A blast of frigid air swept across the sidewalk, making a mushroom of her pleated skirt. In front of an antique store she halted nearly overturning a frail lady in a balaclava. Catching sight of herself in a full-length mirror, she walked towards it, muttering, "My God," then jerked herself upright and backed towards to the middle of the sidewalk, "Can that really be me?" She started to bubble. Her laugh, whinnying, went on a long time. "Only yesterday I was Beauteous Beula," she told the short, broad man walking briskly towards her.

"You interested in a mirror? Come inside. Take a look around. Come an. I'll get you a cup of hot cawfee."

Beula remained on the sidewalk, bent over, face set in a frown. Swallowing, she straightened up and crossed the sidewalk to the store. The owner, bare-armed, his grayish wavy hair well combed, smiled a dealer's smile, "I got more inside. Square, round, oblong, oval. You name the shape I got it. All refinished. Any type of frame you like. You like gilt I got gilt. You like oak frame I got oak. You like bevelled...What do you like? What do you take, regular?"

Beula sleepwalked through the held-open door. Over the head of the owner, she faced beaten-up upholstery and cracked marble. For a second or two she froze, half-closing her eyes. Then something stirred. Heat was coursing through her body, an unpleasant sensation as though her veins were filling with sand and she was about to explode She opened her mouth in a yawn and began to scream at the top of her lungs. The store owner gave a start, his expression shifting from mild contempt to black-browed resentment. He lifted hairy hands to his face and plastered down his immaculate hair.

"Hey," he shouted to make himself heard, "What the hell you think you're playing at? You stop it, you hear, you stop it." He took her by the shoulders and shook her lightly. "That's better, that's better Sit here." He indicated a dining chair and, dusting it, patted the seat. She lowered her head and remained standing.

He handed her the plastic cup and stirrer, "Is cream and sugar okay?"

"Yes," she managed to say, "I prefer skimmed milk but cream will do nicely."

Impressed by her accents, he relaxed, "Sure the city can get ya down. I often feel like squeaming myself," he chuckled, "You gave me a scare, you know that? I don't scare easy." He edged his way out of the cluttered doorway, gently lifted the oval mirror and brought it in, turning it to face her.

The cup fell from Beula's hands. She shuddered and began to scream in earnest and he could not silence her. She ran out of the store, stood a moment under the awning where the mirror had been, then still screaming, moved to the sidewalk holding herself erect, one arm raised like a singer in dramatic *legato*. In between the held high shrieks she made sobbing noises. Soon a knot of passers-by had congregated.

"I believe it's called a paroxysm. I've read about them. Sometimes the patient rolls on the ground. We did a seminar on them in Psychiatry Three."

"I seen her come outta your store, mister, and I want to know what the hell you did to hah?"

"She's looking to buy a mirra. Next thing she's carrying on. She looked *shmeggege* when she came in."

"No, it could be some kind of epileptic fit. Not horizontal and not foaming at the mouth. Comes from oxygen being denied to the brain."

"Lady, lady will you take it easy?"

"Careful, there she goes. Hold her armpits."

"Her head shouldn't rest on my *hammentasche*."

"Well then, like I said it is some kind of fit."

"Take her legs and hold them low otherwise she's gonna kick my face. We gotta find a couch. When I say 'Lift' you lift. Have you got her?"

"I ain't got her."

"I said she's not coming in. I can't have her in my store. I got insurance to think of. She's nothing to do with me."

"I'm gonna call the police."

"What the woman needs is an ambulance, not the police."

"He's right. We gotta call for an ambulance. Hey mister, you got a cushion for her head?"

"Look how she's panting. Is there some water around here?"

"Could be a stroke."

"...example of a psychotic break."

"Hey you, see that cushion? Ease it under her head now."

"Leave her under the awning. She's not coming into my store."

"What's with you?"

"It's more *tsures*."

"Irv, this is an em-er-gen-cy."

"I don't need an emergency. I don't want trouble in my store."

"Our store, Irv."

"Who secured the twenty-five year lease?"

"Who acquires stock? Who makes deliveries?"

"I, Irv Pozzack am fully extended. I don't have insurance for a million dollars."

"Don't hock me a chinick."

"I feel my colon acting up."

*

It had got dark by the time Beula opened her eyes. Stretched out on the sidewalk, head resting on a seat cushion, a dog's dewy nose scattered steamy breaths around her. The dog smelled of old boats. Its spoon-shaped tongue lapped her cheeks, rinsed the stickiness from her eyes and nose. She put up a hand to scratch the dog's ear.

"Augusta, what you doin'? Get over here."

By degrees she raised herself to a sitting position then got to her feet, against the wall between the furniture store and a coffee shop. She inhaled, counting to six, as she straightened up. When her knees started to sag, the dog's owner clutched her under the armpits. The store proprietor watching them from inside, opened the door, carefully threaded her tote bag onto her arm and hurried back in. Reorienting herself against the young man, Beula concentrated on large objects: a white truck bigger than a railcar, the blue and white 104 bus, then on the individual with corkscrew curls holding a curly-headed dog with one arm and herself on the other. In slow motion he tied the dog to a No Waiting sign then led her into the coffee shop.

"Why don't we get you something? You sit there. Let me face the window so I can check nobody tries to steal her." Squeezing himself into the seat, he said, "I'm Septimus, by the way."

Her teeth were chattering, "Hot, hot. I must have something hot. Tea."

He looked astonished, "You don't sound hoarse. Doesn't your throat hurt after all that exercise? You were screaming a long time."

"It's funny but I don't…have…a sore throat."

"Where are you from? England? Why couldn't you collapse there? What are you doing in New York?"

"I came to flee the patriarchal ice. Escape being five inches tall."

The young man half-smiled, half-frowned, "Well, I suppose here you'd have some chance to grow. You might make it to ten inches! Hey Sir! Sir, could we get—what's the soup today? Corn chowder okay? All right, one soup, a bagel and a shmear, one black tea and one regular coffee."

"I felt a rumbling in my chest. Heaving, heaving round and round. Then it erupted. In my head. Next thing up comes the paving stone. I could hear myself."

"The police sure didn't need a radio to find you."

She smiled.

"That's better."

She looked past him to the poodle mix tied to the No Waiting sign.

"Found Augusta out on eastern Long Island, with a broken paw. She didn't bark for days. First I thought her vocal chords were cut. But no, she was abandoned at the end of the summer by some vacation people."

"Like me," Beula said, still smiling, "I was abandoned at the end of a summer." The tea tasted like coconut matting. She turned the teabag over with curiosity, "She must be in seventh heaven."

His expression shifted from solicitude to caution and the silence got awkward.

"I wonder if you'd mind ordering me a cup of coffee and then I ought to go." She held the bagel in both hands, "You're looking at me in a funny way. As if you're afraid I might be interested in you," she broke off a piece of the bagel, "sexually."

He looked up urgently, "Why would you even think something like that?"

"I see warning flashes. Her! On the verge of taking to the streets! Let me set the record straight. You're the last thing on my mind. Your look tells me you think you got signals from me."

"I'm not looking at you any particular way."

"Now you're not. But you were. Pity mingled with disgust."

"I'm showing concern, not disgust."

"I hope so," she drank from the heavy coffee cup, "Secure in your youth and your maleness. Your pale baby face, strong shoulders, thick hair, you poor devil you must think your time's going to stretch to kingdom come."

"Maybe you think your time looks kinda contracted."

Her eyes moved this way and that.

"I've been to prison," he added, "visiting."

"What are you, a social worker?"

"Training to be, specializing in vagrancy. My specialty's inner city areas because problems of relocation are…"

His voice droned on. As he warmed to his theme, she finished the soup and devoured the bagel. When he showed signs of winding down she was quick to butt in with, "So your interest in me's professional!"

"Isn't that senior to sexual interest? You're hardly my generation."

"If we were nearer in age you wouldn't have a chance in hell with me."

"How old are you anyway?"

She shook off the question in a horselike gesture..

"Do you have children?"

"Don't think you can make a role for me to satisfy some fantasy of yours," She drained the cup and nodded for more coffee, "Just because your world looks solid and eternal."

He stared into his glass.

"I'm screaming in the street. For the price of a coffee you want me to get interested in your stupid career. To be your audience?"

He grew glum and remote then roused himself, saying in a too-gentle voice, "I'm trying to help. What do you do?"

In the silence that followed, they heard a Frenchman rebut an argument on the irreversible effects of cholesterol.

Do. Beula turned the concept over.

"But h'Alec, you can 'ave a hegg. h'It won't 'urt you."

"It's not what I do," she replied. "What counts is who I am."

"Can you do gourmet cooking?"

"I hope not."

"What about electric wiring?"

"You must be joking."

"What's your field?"

"I'm sitting on the gate."

"I doubt you're up to taking advice from a callow member of *your* audience but here goes. Cut your hair. Capitalize on your style. Researched right, presented right, Madam, your niche awaits." He flinched as she made a rude noise, "Anybody can play the victim. Why not take it one step further? Get yourself certified."

A grim Beula rose to search out the Ladies Room. On return she noticed the check had disappeared and the young man was outside communing with the dog, Steadying herself against the chair, she fished in her bag for change, and slapped her remaining two dollar bills on the table. At the gutter, she leant on a traffic meter as Septimus untied his joyous dog, and piloted Beula to the corner to wait for the WALK sign.

*

As man and dog melted into the maze of neon, Beula limped along Broadway beneath an orange night sky and dots of many-colored lights. Strollers skirted her, bicycles swerved, vans idled at the turn, shoppers scattered from her path. Groping her way past the A & P, the drugstore, pizza heaven, she began to feel weightless, afloat in the all-engulfing, a fleeting sensation of being everywhere, yet nowhere. Was death's embrace like this?

Henry the doorman eyed her, reached up for two envelopes, placed them in her hand closing it over them, and pushed the elevator button. When the car doors opened, her knees gave way and the two airmail letters fell to the floor. The green uniformed Henry caught her and, gripping her arm, shouted at someone in the lobby. At the second floor, he half-carried, half dragged her along the airless, dimly-lit passage. With one hand he held her against the wall and with the other struggled with her keys. The front door yielded first try. He parked her on the plaid armchair in the tiny hall and, switching on all lights, searched out the telephone. She sat cradling Steno and Yuri, scratching their heads, massaging their necks, wondering how to get up to attend to their needs. After a telephone call to the front desk the doorman hoisted her to her feet, wrenched off the Harrods topcoat and flung it over the armchair. Then getting behind he steered her to the messy bedroom and let her fall face down on the bed, dragging out from under her Jooning's purple flannelette sheet.

43

Beula, coming to, thought she heard a key rattling. Next thing, Emery was in view and the light was hurting her eyes. Emery switched off the bedroom and hall lights, then checked the refrigerator. Both cats, one slight and delicate, the other twice the size and fat, rubbed against Emery's legs while she rinsed cat dishes and found the can-opener

"What's the time?" Beula called.

"Suppertime. I'm sending out for pizza. Are y'interested?"

Beula's eyes flickered, "All right but…no sausage."

"Do you have money?"

Beula shifted her head on the pillow, saying in a dreamy voice, "Will they change a fifty?"

"Forget it. I got singles."

It was a quarter to midnight.

*

Next day about mid-morning, Beula got up from bed and staggered to the living room to the easy chair facing the curtained window. At half

217

past eleven that night Emery stalked in, talking at high speed about the second week of early mornings, late nights and no breaks; her need of forty eight hours sleep; the worry over Tyrone holding out. Making time for laundry and bill paying. That the building she's working on is antique and has fifty units. That the pay she's not complaining about, that Claudine, the big client is talking of putting her in a course on interiors and that she's over-interested in the secret bio-supplies. "Still, she now pays on time," Emery concluded, "Since I acquainted her with how much jerking around I won't tolerate. She knows diddly about the finer details that take the time, like the cutting in. I mean I'm busy all hours and what with putting finishing touches to six apartments, I just haven't been around."

Silence.

"What's up?"

"I followed him here and now he's gone."

"Aha." Emery examined her hands, "But why him? Was he some kind of knockout?"

Beula sighed, "Once said he was knocked out by me. Lavish in his prostration."

"His what?"

"I know how it feels to be a graven image," Beula added, "He had no recall of any of it. As if some other bloke was doing the genuflecting. Our final date was for my birthday. I found a Latino restaurant and ordered the Kettlehole cake."

"What's that?"

Beula propped herself up on one elbow, "Chocolate ring, brushed with white icing. Green jelly in the hollow. I was afraid he wouldn't show but he arrives at four thirty for which they dock me an hour's pay. When the cake with one candle wobbles round the corner he refrains from asking my age. I had decided to duck it in any case. But over coffee this other part of me shouts it out, "The Kettlehole's hit the mid-century." Beula pulled a pillow from the floor, "My memory is of him sitting across from me behind the empties…the last thing he's saying is the high-gloss finish on the table…is…very…practical."

"Looks like we gotta get you on a plane," Emery said.

Beula shook her head, "No ticket."

"Charge it."

"No chargecards."

"Get your family to pay. What are families for?"

"I already owe my mother."

"So?"

"If I borrow more…I'll owe more. And besides," Beula stood up and revolved her shoulders, "There's the quarantine. Cat boarding over six months. Costly to me and hard on them."

"You can pay it all back."

"With what?"

"All right," Emery grunted, "Gimme the fifty and I'll do my best to change it. Where's your pocket book?"

"Look in the top drawer."

Emery shouted from the bedroom, "No pocket book…It's where?. Wrapped in—what? A headscarf. Okay." She reappeared holding up the fifty dollar bill, "This is rent money, right? Yeah the rent's due this Friday."

"No, it's this month's."

"This month's? You mean you've been spending the rent?"

"So far nothing's been said."

The buzzer sounded.and Emery dashed out. She reappeared looking solemn and, whistling through her teeth, threw a large pizza wheel and the change on the bed.

"I know what you're going to ask," Beula cried, "But I can't help you out. Even if I felt up to it".

"With the right person I'd go fifty-fifty. But I can't find the right person."

"If I felt right I still couldn't do it. Never held a paintbrush in my life. The nearest I got was an evening course on the use of space in a bedsitter."

They each took a wedge of pizza and bit into it, pulling out strings of cheese for the cats.

*

"On this side of the building the john has the best view of the river. Take a look around and see if you're up to doing a patch. You might feel you could roller part of a wall while I start on the master suite."

"My head's still swimming a bit."

"OK, sit on this chair and use this roller. Paint only down to here. Are you up to trying that? White over peach. And be careful! Stop six inches short of the oak surrounds for me to cut in," Emery heaved a plank into the master bedroom then made trips back for two of the three stepladders.

Beula, on a portable kitchen stool next to a roll of tarpaulin, sat clutching her head. Then, rousing herself, she noticed the smell of apples cooking. Carefully she got down on the floor, opened the paint can, found a stained pallet and stirred the paint innumerable times. Hunching her shoulders, she removed the roller from its linen wrapping and peered at the wall. Very slowly she poured paint into the pan. Dousing the roller and shaking loose drops she approached the small patch of peach wall closest at hand. Then she began stretching. Higher and higher. By the time she had rollered one wall except for the cutting in areas, she became aware of two things. One, that aroma of stewed apples on the stove turned out to be the paint, and Two, that repetitive motion releases the mind. Again she felt weightless, floating in space. By the time she had turned to the second wall she was looking down on herself inspecting the Bogota apartment's white walls, satisfied that her choice of Sicilian Umber toned in with the avocado carpet. Tackling the corner next to the oak-framed window, an image of Jeremy joined in, sprawled on the orange sofa, head behind arms, eyes clouded. While she noted his fine-striped rumpled shirt, his wide brown hands, greasy nails, she had covered all four walls, one foot from all edges.

In bewilderment she stepped back, checking for traces of peach showing through. With the roller soaking in soapy water, she unwrapped Emery's number one brush and ran her thumb over it. Thoughtfully she dipped into the unlabelled paint can, lined the brush up against the oak door jamb and, holding it parallel, drew it away from the edge, following the line of the door up to the transom. As she worked from the spare stepladder's third rung and completed the cutting in of the two window frames, the image had long gone and she had surrendered herself to the sheer heaven of the all engulfing.

At one fifteen, Emery shakily descended the main stepladder, checked the soles of her sneakers, immersed brushes and rollers in soapy water and squished them around, then produced the silver hammer for closing paint cans. With her radio announcing a broadcast from Sadlers Wells, she shook out a length of towelling and, groaning, lay flat on the floor to stretch all sections of the spine.

At one thirty Beula jumped when Emery tapped her shoulder in time to Tchaikowsky's 'Sleeping Beauty.'

"Lunch did you say? What time is it?"

Emery bent down to scrutinize the baseboard then straightened up and backed to the center of the room. "Y'know those lower walls look really really…" she wheeled round, "Hey, Claudine," she cried, "Come here and take a look at this. I must say it's…In fact I'd say it's…Well, you finished the cutting in and…I mean, hey you did the whole parlor. I am totally flabbergasted!"

"I must have been here quite a while."

"It's so even!" they chorused..

Against the wall Beula murmured, "There's just this patch. I'll finish the room up, put the brush in soak and catch up with you."

"Lunch is on us. We'll be at Gitlitz".

"How come you hardly, I mean you never spilled a drop?" Emery called over her shoulder.

Beula pulled hair out of her eyes, "This may sound crazy but the hang of it comes from the last place you'd expect it." Dipping the broad, straight-edged brush into the paintpot she trimmed, then lining it up flat and horizontal to ensure an even spread, shut her eyes and the line between wall and baseboard was perfect.

About the Author

*B*arbara P. Parsons was born in Portsmouth England, to a naval family. After working overseas in many different lands, including the venue of much of this novel, Colombia, she came to the U.S. with her American husband in 1973. She is active in green and animal liberation issues, has contributed articles to Sierra Club Wildlife Involvement News and edits the UFETA (Unitarians for Ethical Treatment of Animals) newsletter. A chapter from Beula Kettlehole appeared in Humerus Magazine. This is her first novel.